A Note from Stephanie about Christmas Fun

Everyone loves Christmas vacation, right? Wrong! I *didn't* love it when my best friend was spending *our* winter break with a cute, fun, guitar-playing boy! Of course, James asked Allie *and* me to show him the sights. But my Great-Aunt Sophie was in town. Guess who was supposed to show her around? Leaving guess-who alone with James? Guess right and you'll know why two girls plus one boy didn't add up to major fun. Until things worked out in a very surprising way. But before I explain about that, let me explain about my very surprising family.

Right now there are nine people and a dog living in our house—and for all I know, someone new could move in at any time. There's me, my big sister, D.J., my little sister, Michelle, and my dad, Danny. But that's just the beginning.

When my mom died, Dad needed help. So he asked his old college buddy, Joey Gladstone, and my Uncle Jesse to come live with us, to help take care of me and my sisters.

Back then, Uncle Jesse didn't know much about taking care of three little girls. He was more into rock 'n' roll. Joey didn't know anything about kids, either—but it sure was funny watching him learn!

Having Uncle Jesse and Joey around was like

having three dads instead of one! But then something even better happened—Uncle Jesse fell in love. He married Rebecca Donaldson, Dad's co-host on his TV show, *Wake Up, San Francisco*. Aunt Becky's so nice—she's more like a big sister than an aunt.

Next Uncle Jesse and Aunt Becky had twin baby boys. Their names are Nicky and Alex, and they are adorable!

I love being part of a big family. Still, things can get pretty crazy when you live in such a full house!

FULL HOUSE™: Stephanie novels

Available from MINSTREL Books

FULL HOUSE™
Stephanie

Two-for-One
Christmas Fun

Peter Landesman

A Parachute Press Book

A
MINSTREL®
BOOK

Published by POCKET BOOKS
New York   London   Toronto   Sydney   Tokyo   Singapore

A MINSTREL PAPERBACK *Original*

A Minstrel Book published by
POCKET BOOKS, a division of Simon & Schuster Inc.
1230 Avenue of the Americas, New York, NY 10020

A PARACHUTE PRESS BOOK

READING Copyright © 1995 by Warner Bros. Television

FULL HOUSE, characters, names and all related indicia are trademarks of Warner Bros. Television © 1995.

ISBN: 0-671-53546-3

First Minstrel Books printing December 1995

10 9 8 7 6 5 4 3 2 1

A MINSTREL BOOK and colophon are registered trademarks of Simon & Schuster Inc.

Cover photo by Schultz Photography

Printed in the U.S.A.

CHAPTER
1

◆ ◂ ◼ ◆

"Hey, Allie, it's official," Stephanie Tanner said happily. She checked her watch as she hopped off the school bus. "As of this very second we're on Christmas vacation!"

"You've got that right," Allie Taylor said. "It's too good to be true. No more finals to worry about, no more papers. Even my backpack feels lighter."

"That's because it *is* lighter, Allie," Stephanie pointed out. "You're not carrying any books in it!"

"Oh, right," Allie said. "No homework either!" Allie's green eyes danced as she reached up to tuck a lock of wavy brown hair behind one ear. Stephanie and Allie had been best friends for eight years—ever since their kindergarten teacher had sat them next to one another. Allie could be shy around boys, but she was also down-to-earth, loyal, and fun to be with.

"I still can't believe how lucky we are that the school board decided to repaint the school," Allie said.

"Yeah," Stephanie agreed. "And we get a whole extra week off this year. That means lots of time— starting *now*," Stephanie reminded Allie, "to have the best vacation ever."

"Since you seem to have it all figured out," Allie began, "why don't you share your master plans with me? What are we going to do, besides miss Darcy and think about how jealous we are that she's off skiing and we're still stuck at home?"

Darcy Powell was Stephanie's other best friend. Darcy was tall and graceful and everyone always said she looked like Whitney Houston's younger sister. With her curly dark hair and dark eyes, she was definitely one of the cutest girls in Lakeview Middle School. The three of them—Stephanie, Allie, and Darcy—usually did everything together. But this year Darcy's parents had planned a special family trip to Aspen. They'd picked up Darcy right after her last class and headed straight for the airport.

"We don't have to be that jealous of Darcy,"

Stephanie said as she and Allie walked to her house. "There's still lots we can do. First, we can go to the mall and get all our Christmas shopping done."

"But we go to the mall almost every weekend," Allie pointed out. "That's not all that exciting."

"It will be exciting after we drop lots of very subtle hints to each other about what we want for Christmas," Stephanie replied, "such as the new Counting Crows video I've been dying to own, hint, hint."

"Right." Allie smiled. "And then we can go to the indoor skating rink—so I can try out those new ice skates that I didn't get for Christmas last year, hint, hint."

"Give me a better hint, Allie," Stephanie suggested. "Ice skates would wipe out my entire gift fund. I still have to buy something for Darcy, and a family present."

"Have you all picked names yet?" Allie asked.

Stephanie knew Allie was referring to the great Tanner family Christmas tradition—Secret Santa. There were nine people in Stephanie's family. They had realized long ago that there was only one way to save themselves from going broke each Christmas. They decided that each person would buy only one present. Every year, they put all their

3

names in a hat. There were Stephanie and her two sisters, D.J. and Michelle, their father, Danny, Uncle Jesse and his wife, Becky, and Joey Gladstone, Danny's friend from college. Even the four-year-old twins, Nicky and Alex, were included. Then everyone picked a name and that was who they bought a Christmas present for. Although everybody knew that the twins never bought presents themselves. Poor Becky and Jesse—they got stuck buying four presents instead of just two.

"No, we didn't pick the names yet," Stephanie replied. "Maybe this week."

"Well, hope for one of the twins," Allie suggested. "Little kids are happy with inexpensive gifts. Like you could get them a King Mojo Komodo action figure."

"Who is he?" Stephanie asked, stopping short.

"You don't know King Mojo—?" Allie began.

"Not him. *Him*—" Stephanie's eyes were riveted on something ahead of her. "Allie, I think we've just changed our Christmas plans. Forget skating and shopping. Everything's on hold. We need to find out some very important information."

"About what?" Allie asked. "The good Christmas sales at Brisbee's Department Stores?"

"Who cares about sales?" Stephanie cried, pointing. "I'm talking about an incredibly cute guy! The

4

one who just got out of the car in front of my house."

Allie glanced up and saw who Stephanie was pointing to. She let out a deep sigh.

Stephanie nodded in agreement. This boy certainly deserved a sigh. He was tall and handsome with sandy brown hair that curled up at his neck. He was wearing a plaid flannel shirt with rolled-up sleeves, faded jeans, and dark brown leather Doc Marten boots. And he was unloading a suitcase from the back of a minivan that was parked right in front of the Tanners' house.

"He's gorgeous," Allie whispered. "Who is he?"

"That's what I just asked you. If this was the most absolutely awesome Christmas ever, he'd be a surprise present from my very best friend in the world," Stephanie joked. "But I know you don't have anything to do with it. And Darcy's thirty thousand feet in the air right now. So it must be a simple case of fate."

"He must be visiting someone around here," Allie said.

"Well, let's go and find out," Stephanie said. "Maybe he can end up visiting us!"

Stephanie and Allie dropped their book bags on the Tanners' front porch and hurried over to the van. They stood there for a few minutes, each waiting for the other to speak first to the cute guy.

Allie elbowed Stephanie to say something. Stephanie opened her mouth, but no words came out. Then, just as the boy turned around, Allie elbowed Stephanie a little harder.

"Hey!" Stephanie yelped—partly from Allie's nudging and partly from how cute the boy was up close. He looked at least fifteen. "I mean hi," she added with a grin.

The boy laughed. Stephanie said quickly, "My name's Stephanie and this is Allie."

"I'm James," the boy said. "James O'Brien."

"Nice to meet you, James." Allie smiled.

"O'Brien?" Stephanie asked. "Are you related to my neighbors?"

"If the O'Briens are your neighbors, then I am," James said. "They're my aunt and uncle. My family decided to come out west this year. We've had enough white Christmases at home in New Hampshire."

"That's great," Stephanie blurted out. She knew she was blushing and hoped it wasn't too noticeable.

"I hope so," James said. "I've always wanted to check out San Francisco." He pulled a guitar from the back of the minivan and slung it over his shoulder. "So what exciting plans do you two have for vacation?" James asked. "Maybe you can tell me all the great places to go around here."

"Funny you should ask," Stephanie replied slowly. Suddenly, her mind was a blank. *What are the great places around here?* she thought. *We can't just say the mall and the movies or we'll seem totally boring!* Stephanie looked at Allie for help.

"Yeah," Allie added, stalling for time. "We were just discussing our vacation plans when we saw you unpacking."

"Oh," James said, "are you guys busy for your whole vacation?" He looked a little disappointed.

"No, we're not at all busy," Stephanie said hastily.

"Nope," Allie agreed.

"In fact, we don't have any plans at all," Stephanie added, not wanting James to think they were too busy for him.

"Well, we do have plans," Allie said quickly, shooting Stephanie a look. "Sort of."

Stephanie realized she sounded like a total loser by saying they had no plans. "Well, actually," she hastily added, "we're planning to do the usual. You know, the mall, movies—"

"The ice rink," Allie added.

"How about clubs?" James asked hopefully.

"Any good places to hear music around here?" He tapped his guitar case.

"Well," Stephanie tried again. She stared at Allie desperately. They'd probably blown any chance of hanging out with James. It was so obvious that they didn't know anything about the cool places to go. Stephanie didn't want to admit that they weren't really allowed to do that kind of stuff.

"There's one place," Stephanie began casually, "but I haven't been there in so long, I kind of forgot the name—"

James smiled broadly and shrugged. "Don't worry about it," he said kindly. "I've got a better idea. Why don't we combine our Christmas plans and go find the action together?" He looked at Stephanie and Allie and raised his eyebrows. "Like, how about tomorrow night?" he asked.

Allie's jaw dropped, but she closed it when Stephanie stepped down hard on her toe.

"You bet," Stephanie said excitedly. "That's a great plan."

"Yeah," Allie added quickly. "That'll be fun."

"Good." James smiled, picking up his suitcase.

"So, should we call you?" Allie asked nervously.

"Or do you want to call us?" Stephanie added.

"Or do you think we should just, like, set a time now?" Allie suggested.

"How about we just talk tomorrow during the day?" James suggested, nodding at Stephanie's house and the O'Briens's. "It's not like we're that far away."

"Of course," Stephanie said. "I mean, right. You know where I live. Just come over anytime."

"Bye, Stephanie, Allie," James said as he turned away. "See you tomorrow."

"Yeah, see ya!" Stephanie called.

"Bye!" Allie added.

The girls gazed at each other excitedly.

"Whatever you do," Stephanie whispered, grabbing Allie by the arm and squeezing her, "just don't squeal or giggle or scream—until we get inside."

Allie nodded silently. Her eyes shining.

"I think this *is* going to be the absolutely very best Christmas ever," Stephanie predicted.

"James is so cute." Stephanie giggled as she and Allie sat at her kitchen table with a steaming hot pizza between them.

"And friendly," Allie added as she reached for a slice and slid it onto her plate. "Do you think we should invite him over for pizza now?" she asked suddenly.

"Let's not push it," Stephanie suggested. "It's

already amazing that he wants to hang out with us. *And* go to clubs and listen to music. We don't want to overkill on the first day."

"He's so cool!" Allie said for the tenth time.

"He must be fifteen, don't you think?" Stephanie guessed. "Maybe fourteen, but a mature fourteen."

"This will be better than skiing!" Allie said. "Just wait till we tell Darcy all about him."

"Speaking of Darcy, let's go to the mall tomorrow, early, and pick out a present for her," Stephanie said.

"Sure, and then we can see a matinee of that new sci-fi movie," Allie agreed.

"We should get her something fantastic," Stephanie said, pulling another piece of gooey pizza from the box and wrapping the cheese around her finger before popping it into her mouth.

Stephanie looked up as her father, Danny, entered the room. Her younger sister, Michelle, was with him. They were both carrying grocery bags.

"Hel*lo* there, girls." Danny grinned. "I see you're eating a healthy holiday meal?" He raised an eyebrow at them.

"Don't I get any pizza?" Michelle asked, holding out a plate.

"Michelle, this pizza is for Allie and me," Stephanie explained. Danny turned from the counter to give her a stern look. Stephanie sighed and handed Michelle a piece of pizza.

"Oh, pizza!" D.J. rushed into the kitchen. "I thought I smelled pizza. But I thought I was making it up. With all my studying, I've worked up a real appetite." D.J. was Stephanie's older sister. For the past few days she'd been studying like crazy for her college exams.

"This is just what I need for a study break," D.J. said as she grabbed a plate from the cupboard. "You don't mind, do you, Steph? Allie?" D.J. slid a piece of pizza onto her plate and leaned against the counter.

Stephanie and Allie looked at each other and shrugged.

Meanwhile Michelle had picked all the pepperoni off her pizza and put it back in the carton. "You should have gotten extra cheese," she said with her mouth full.

"We should have gotten extra pizza," Stephanie said. She eyed the last slice on the table. "Or else we should have had this delivered to your house," she whispered to Allie.

"By the way, I'm glad all of you girls are here," Danny said, "because I have some news."

"Uh-oh," D.J. groaned. "That's almost never a good start."

"We'll be having a visitor this vacation," Danny continued. "Your aunt Sophie is coming all the way from Europe for a visit."

"Who's she?" Stephanie asked.

"Actually, she's my great-aunt," Danny explained, "on the Tanner side. And technically, she's your great-great-aunt, but once you get up to one *great* you don't add any more. It's more polite, and won't make her feel so old. In fact, you should all probably just call her Aunt Sophie."

"How do I know if she's so great when I've never even met her?" Michelle asked.

"I don't remember her at all," Stephanie admitted.

"I guess I don't talk about her much," Danny agreed. "She's been living in Europe for a long long time. And it has been eleven years since you last saw her."

"Eleven years!" Michelle cried. "I wasn't even born yet!"

"I don't even remember if I remember her," D.J. said.

"Anyway, girls, her holiday plans fell through and so I've invited her here. Christmas is the time for families to be together, after all. She'll be flying in tomorrow night, and I'll need you two to come to the airport with me."

Suddenly Stephanie felt a little sick. "Which two?" she asked, horrified that she knew the answer.

"You and Michelle, of course," Danny said. "It'll be nice for her to be met by the family, and I know she's looking forward to seeing you again, Stephanie."

"But why me?" Stephanie cried, staring at Allie. "Tomorrow night is no good."

"Because everyone else is busy," Danny explained. "Becky has to take care of some details at the TV station, which means that your uncle Jesse will have to take care of the twins. Joey has a comedy show to do, and D.J. has to study for her big exams."

"Sorry, Stephanie," D.J. added. "Got to study!"

Stephanie could tell that D.J. wasn't all that sorry. How many times would she get away with using studying as an excuse? Stephanie wondered. *She probably stays in college just to get out of all the boring things I'm forced to do*, Stephanie thought.

Grabbing the last piece of pizza, Stephanie tried one more time. "But can't Great-Great-Aunt Sophie see me when she gets back here? I've already made plans with Allie to—"

"Let's just skip the 'greats,' Stephanie," Danny

interrupted. "And I'm sorry, honey, but she hasn't seen you in a long time."

"I know!" Stephanie cried. "It's already been eleven years. So why can't it be eleven years and one more day?"

"Stephanie, she'll be here only a week," Danny said sternly. "I'm sorry to cancel your plans, but you don't see Aunt Sophie very often. I think you can make the sacrifice. You'll still have another week of vacation to spend with Allie *after* Christmas."

"But, Dad—"

"That's it, Stephanie," Danny said.

Stephanie couldn't believe it. She gazed at Allie sadly. So much for their big date with James. Now the absolutely very best Christmas was becoming an absolute disaster!

CHAPTER
2

◆ ◀ ◆ ◆

D.J. left the kitchen to go back to her studying. Danny went upstairs to help Michelle clean up her room.

"I can't believe he's doing this to me," Stephanie said as soon as her family had gone. She dropped the piece of pizza she'd been holding back into the box. It was cold anyway. And the cheese looked rubbery. Stephanie had completely lost her appetite.

"Is it going to take all night to go to the airport?" Allie asked. "Maybe we can do something after?"

Stephanie shook her head. "I know my dad. He's on a roll. It's going to be an entire night of family fun—I can just tell."

"What are you going to talk to an old lady about anyway?" Allie wondered.

"Exactly," Stephanie complained, glumly resting her chin in her hand. "I'm probably going to have to sit around and listen to her talk about the last time she saw me . . . when I was *two!* I can hear it now: 'My, how you've grown, Stephanie.' "

"Sounds awful," Allie agreed, picking at a piece of pizza crust. "I can't believe you're going to miss going out for that," she said.

"Yeah," Stephanie sighed. "Just when vacation was looking so good. I'm sorry, Allie. I guess this means we'll have to cancel our music date with James."

"Oh," Allie said, suddenly falling silent. "Yeah, I guess so . . . ," she agreed after a moment. "We'll just have to do it some other time. It's all right."

Danny bounded through the kitchen door again. "I hope you girls are finished with your pizza," he said. "We don't have much time to get the house shipshape for Aunt Sophie." He smiled. "Think you could give me a little help?"

Danny reached under the sink for a sponge. "I'm going to clean the oven. D.J. will iron the tablecloth and napkins—when she's done studying, that is. Michelle will put away the rest of the groceries. And, Stephanie, you can start polishing the silver

16

candlesticks, while Allie begins filing all those coupons in alphabetical—"

"Dad," Stephanie interrupted. "Allie doesn't live here. You can't include her."

"Oh, right," Danny agreed. "Sorry, Allie." He put a list under a magnet on the refrigerator door and said, "Don't forget to check off your job after you've done it, girls."

"Don't worry, Allie," Stephanie said as they stood up. "You don't have to do anything."

"That's okay—" Allie began.

"Well, if you don't mind," Danny said quickly, "maybe you can pick up those pizza crusts before the dog comes in here—"

"You'd better get out of here, Allie," Stephanie interrupted. She grabbed Allie's coat from the back of her chair and pushed it into her arms. "Now! Unless you really *want* to brush up on your alphabetizing skills."

"Sorry I can't stay to help," Allie said.

"That's okay, I understand," Stephanie said as she walked Allie to the front door.

Opening the door for Allie, Stephanie took a peek at the house next door. She wondered what James was up to. She handed Allie her book bag and said, "With all the people in this house, why am I always the one who gets stuck doing the junky family stuff?"

"Look at it this way," Allie consoled her friend. "If you're hanging out at your house, at least you can keep an eye on James."

"Not if my father is in one of his cleaning frenzies, I can't. His list of chores for me is probably longer than Michelle's Christmas list."

Allie giggled. "We are still on for the mall, aren't we?"

"You bet!" Stephanie cried. "If I have to spend the whole night with Aunt Sophie, I'm going to spend the day with you!"

"Good." Allie smiled. "My mom and I will pick you up right after breakfast."

"Don't be late," Stephanie added. "We'll have *major* fun!"

The next morning Stephanie jumped into the car with Allie and her mom. She was ready to shop!

"How did the rest of the cleanup go?" Allie asked.

"Not too badly, I guess," Stephanie admitted. "After the candlesticks, all I had to do was clean between the tiles in the shower—with a toothbrush—and arrange all the shampoo bottles in size order."

Allie tried to hold back her giggles until Stephanie started chuckling herself. Then the two of them doubled over with laughter.

"Sometimes it makes me crazy what a neat freak my dad is," Stephanie muttered. "I don't know where he got it from. I just hope he hasn't passed it on to me."

"Don't worry," Allie offered. "I've been your friend forever, and you've never been neat."

"Thanks a lot," Stephanie replied, rolling her eyes.

"Hey, it's true," Allie went on. "Remember the last time you opened your locker at school? Kids thought it was the recycling bin and started throwing their trash into it."

"Somehow, you always help me see the bright side of things," Stephanie said. She grinned at Allie.

A few minutes later Allie's mom pulled up in front of the mall and the two girls hopped out of the car. Allie promised they'd meet her mother back at the same door after the movie.

"So now that we're here, what are we going to buy for Darcy?" Allie asked as she and Stephanie went inside. "Since there are two of us, maybe we should chip in and get something really super?"

They went to the sports store. Darcy loved to

ski. They spent almost an hour there. Then Stephanie and Allie realized that Darcy already had all the mittens and matching caps she would ever need. They needed a break in the food court. Maybe some bagels and iced tea would help them brainstorm for a better present. There were a few other kids from school there, and after chatting for a while, Stephanie and Allie decided to wander over to the music store. Maybe they could get something for Darcy there.

"This was a great idea," Stephanie said, her nose up against the store window. "Look who's here!"

There in the first row of the pop/rock section was James O'Brien! He was wearing a long-sleeved gray T-shirt rolled up to his elbows. Stephanie and Allie hurried in, but Stephanie suddenly stopped at the row of golden oldies.

"We can't just run up to him," Stephanie explained in a hushed tone. "We'll look too silly."

"But, Stephanie, isn't it also silly to pretend that we don't see him?" Allie asked. "We have a date with him tonight, after all. It's not as though we're strangers."

"It's better if we just casually bump into each other," Stephanie argued. "Trust me."

"I don't know—" Allie began.

"Hey, you two!" James suddenly said, coming

over to them. "Stephanie, Allie, what's up? What are you guys buying?" James asked. He leaned over to get a better glimpse of the CD Stephanie had picked up.

Stephanie gazed down and realized she was holding on to an old Frank Sinatra CD. She felt her face turn red.

"Do you really listen to him?" James asked.

"Well, actually—" Stephanie began.

"It's for her father!" Allie finished quickly.

"Right," Stephanie agreed. *Thank you, Allie,* she said silently. *Now I really am going to get you the best present ever!* "He loves this mushy old stuff," Stephanie explained.

"What are you buying?" Allie asked.

"The Crash Test Dummies," James said, showing them the CD in his hands. "Though I like folk music too."

"They're both great," Allie agreed.

"What kind of music are you into?" James asked Stephanie.

"Counting Crows, U2, the Cranberries," Stephanie said.

"We definitely will like the same groups," James said eagerly. "That'll make it easy when we go out tonight."

"Speaking of tonight . . ." Allie started to say.

"Oh, right," Stephanie said sadly. "I'm really sorry, James, but we can't go out. I have a relative coming into town and I have to go to the airport."

"That's too bad, Stephanie," James said. He seemed genuinely disappointed. Then he glanced at Allie and his face lit up. "What about you, Allie? Can't you still go?"

"Uh," Allie stammered, and her face turned red. She gazed back and forth from Stephanie to James for a moment. "Well, if Stephanie can't go, I guess I can't either," she finally answered.

"Oh, that's okay," James said. "Some other time."

"How about the ice rink?" Allie asked quickly. "We can go tomorrow night if you want?"

"That would be great," James agreed. "Stephanie? Are you in?"

"Definitely," Stephanie replied firmly. *Even if I have to sneak out a window to get there*, she added silently.

"Great!" James said. "But I'd better warn you that I'm not a very good skater."

"That's okay," Stephanie said. *He's probably just being modest*, she thought to herself. She couldn't imagine James being bad at anything. "We're not so great either," she added.

"Oh, I'm sure you're a whole lot better than

me," James added with a smile. "You look like the athletic type."

Stephanie smiled back, feeling flattered at the compliment.

"But we should still do the music thing sometime," James added as he started for the register with his CD. "You'll have to come by my aunt and uncle's house some night soon and hear me play guitar. Deal?"

"You bet," Stephanie agreed.

"You too, Allie," he added.

They watched him as he paid for his disc, then waved good-bye as he left the store.

"I think he likes you," Allie said as soon as he had disappeared around a corner.

"I think he likes *you*," Stephanie disagreed. "He especially said 'you too' when he left."

"Yeah, but every time he looked at you he smiled," Allie pointed out as they left the store themselves.

"But you're the one who asked him to go skating," Stephanie argued, "so he probably thinks you like him."

"Maybe," Allie admitted, "but I think he was asking you to go over to his house to hear him play guitar."

"I think he was asking us both," Stephanie decided finally as she and Allie headed over to the cinema. "Anyway, it doesn't matter," Stephanie said after a moment. "He's really cute and really nice, and we both get to hang out with him and have an excellent vacation!"

After the matinee, Allie's mom picked them up, dropping Stephanie off at home just in time to leave for the airport.

"Okay, everyone," Danny said as Stephanie climbed into the car. "Seat belts on. Lights. Mirrors. Air bags. Michelle, check the dashboard for the first aid kit."

"Dad," Stephanie sighed. "It's still there, where it always is."

"Right," Danny said as he put the car in gear and backed out of the driveway. "But it always pays to check. Now, girls, about Aunt Sophie. I just want you to be prepared, because she is a little eccentric."

"What does that mean?" Michelle asked.

"That means she likes things that other people don't necessarily like," Danny explained. "But, as I recall, she's also got the Tanner neat-freak genes in her," he added with admiration. "So she'll be just like one of the family."

Stephanie sighed from the backseat. She didn't really care how neat Aunt Sophie would be. After all, it was impossible for anyone to be more of a neat freak than her father.

"That's great," Stephanie said. "She'll probably really enjoy spending time with all of you, then."

"Oh? Where will you be?" Danny asked.

"Well, I have lots of plans for this vacation," Stephanie answered. Her stomach suddenly tied itself in a knot.

"But I told you, I want Aunt Sophie to spend time with the whole family," Danny said. "And that includes you, Steph."

"But, Dad, I already canceled one date to go to the airport tonight. Don't tell me I have to give up more of my plans?"

"Family comes first," Danny replied. "Especially at Christmas. You know how I feel about that."

Stephanie sat the rest of the ride in silence. *I've got better things to do than hang out with an old great-aunt*, Stephanie argued to herself. *Like hang out with Allie—and James.*

She looked out the car window as the lights of the airport landing strips came into view. *And I am going to hang out with them*, she vowed silently. *One way or another.*

CHAPTER
3

◆ ◀ ◆ ◆

At the airport, Stephanie, Michelle, and Danny pushed their way through throngs of people. They were supposed to meet Aunt Sophie's flight from Europe at the customs gate.

"Look," Stephanie suddenly cried. She pointed at a gate up ahead. "Those people are going to Aspen. That's where Darcy is skiing!" Stephanie felt a pang of envy. Darcy was having fun on her vacation. But Stephanie had to give up an evening with James to be crushed by about a million people.

After being elbowed all over her body, Stephanie was having a hard time getting into the holiday spirit. Of course Michelle wasn't having the same problem; she was short enough to keep out of the way of flying shoulder bags and waving arms.

"Okay, girls," Danny said. He paused to smooth out the wrinkle in his shirt as he was jostled by the crowd. "This is where we'll meet Aunt Sophie. Make sure you smile when you see her," he reminded them.

"But, Dad," Stephanie pointed out, "we've seen only old photos of her. How will we recognize her?"

"Well, she looks like a Tanner," Danny replied. "Don't worry, I'm sure you'll know her right away."

Stephanie craned her neck. The people coming through customs were mostly couples and families. They all grasped mountains of luggage. Everywhere she looked, Stephanie saw carry-on bags bulging with brightly wrapped presents.

Then Stephanie noticed a very beautiful and elegant-looking woman. Her shoulder-length gray hair curled over the top of a dramatic black cape. She seemed to be on her own.

Wow, is she glamorous! Stephanie thought. Then the woman turned and began walking in their direction. *She definitely looks like a Tanner*, Stephanie thought excitedly. *She must be Aunt Sophie!*

"Ahh, Aunt Sophie," Danny suddenly called

out. He had a big smile on his face. But he walked right past the beautiful woman with the cape. Then Stephanie saw who he was really speaking to. Her jaw dropped. Her father had wrapped his arms around a funny-looking little woman with a puffy beehive of bluish-gray hair.

That's what a Tanner looks like? Stephanie thought, horrified. *No way!*

Aunt Sophie had all kinds of luggage. Besides her suitcase, she wore a backpack. Plus an oversize bag was slung over one shoulder. She was trying to clutch two tote bags in one hand, and her other hand was pulling a traveling case on wheels.

"I just hate flying!" Stephanie heard her cry out. "Plane schedules are never to be trusted!"

"Oh, Aunt Sophie," Danny teased, checking his watch. "The plane was only three minutes late."

"Exactly!" she said. "That's exactly what I mean!"

Stephanie cringed. *Dad was right about one thing. This woman sure loves punctuality*, Stephanie thought. *I just hope she doesn't expect me to always be on time. Not while I'm on Christmas vacation!*

"Oh, Stephanie!" Aunt Sophie cried as she dropped all of her belongings in front of Michelle. "It's so nice to see you!" Aunt Sophie leaned down and pinched one of Michelle's cheeks. "Hmm," she murmured. "Isn't that something. You still look just like that two-year-old girl I remember so well."

"Umm, Aunt Sophie? That's Michelle," Stephanie tried to point out kindly as she stepped forward. "I'm Stephanie."

"Oh. What a relief," Aunt Sophie said with a huge sigh as she put her hand to her cheek. "I thought you were awfully short for a thirteen-year-old," she said to Michelle. "Of course, I would never have mentioned your height predicament."

"I have a predicament?" Michelle asked worriedly. "Is that like a rash?" Michelle checked her arms and legs.

"Not at all, honey," Danny assured her.

Aunt Sophie kissed Michelle and Stephanie on the cheek. Then she looked Stephanie over from head to toe and said, "You really have grown up, haven't you?"

Stephanie nodded and smiled sweetly, all the while thinking to herself, *Tell that to my father, would you, please? Then maybe he'll let me decide how to spend my time!*

"Do you have any more luggage?" Danny asked Aunt Sophie.

"Oh, no." Aunt Sophie seemed offended. "I always pack very lightly," she told him, lifting her head proudly.

You've got to be kidding! Stephanie thought as she struggled to lift some of the heavy bags.

"Are we going to eat?" Aunt Sophie asked abruptly. "I'm starving. The food on the plane was simply awful," she complained. "And I'd hate to miss my usual six P.M. meal."

"Of course, Aunt Sophie," Danny said soothingly, taking her tote bags and handing them to Stephanie and Michelle. "We thought we'd go right to dinner," he said. "Anywhere you'd like. Michelle suggested a Mexican restaurant we know, and Stephanie suggested an Italian restaurant—"

"Chinese it is," Aunt Sophie declared. "I don't much like Mexican, and I've had so much Italian food, I'm almost sick to death of it. I'd just as soon not have it while I'm here."

Great—that's only one of my *favorite meals*, Stephanie thought. She let Danny, Aunt Sophie, and Michelle walk ahead as they made their way out to the parking lot. Vacation was looking worse and worse by the minute.

Stephanie, Danny, Michelle, and Aunt Sophie were all settled around a table at the Golden Wok. They each had an enormous red menu open in front of them.

"Can I help you?" the waiter asked.

"Hmm," Aunt Sophie murmured. She gave the waiter a long look up and down. She glanced at Stephanie and winked. "Only if you can fit yourself into a fortune cookie," she replied, laughing at her own joke.

The waiter smiled, but Stephanie felt like crawling under the table. The waiter was a cute-looking college-aged guy. She couldn't believe her aunt was flirting with him!

"I've been to China, you know," Aunt Sophie continued. "I had a brilliant Chinese teacher, a wonderful man." Aunt Sophie patted her puff of hair and sighed. "I was fluent in weeks."

"I'll have the sweet and sour chicken," Danny told the waiter.

"And I want the spaghetti noodles," Michelle added.

"That's lo mein," Aunt Sophie corrected her. "Wait!" she cried as the waiter began scribbling. "Let me, please." Aunt Sophie cleared her throat dramatically. "Ahh, xing hai mu xu gao pan gai som sah?"

"Aunt Sophie?" Danny asked worriedly, leaning over and slapping her on the back. "Are you okay? Michelle, give her some water!"

"She's not choking, Dad," Stephanie explained,

her face burning with embarrassment. "She's trying to order—in Chinese."

"Oh." Danny nodded and smiled. "Of course."

But the waiter was still standing there, a blank expression on his face, his pencil poised over his pad.

"I guess my Chinese is a little rusty, huh?" Aunt Sophie asked, clearing her throat. "Fine, then, we'll just do it in English: number 24, number 57, and number 63."

"I think mine's 58," Stephanie interjected.

"Numbers 57 and 58." Aunt Sophie sighed. "You see how easy it is to get confused."

"Yes, ma'am." The waiter nodded and hurried away.

"It sounds so unappetizing like that." Aunt Sophie fussed. "I mean, who wants to eat number 24?"

"*Fried squid in garlic sauce?*" Michelle read. "Ugh. Who's eating that?"

"Well, you, of course," Aunt Sophie said.

"No way!" Michelle cried. "I'm number 42."

"We didn't get a 42," Stephanie pointed out.

"It's just a simple mistake," Danny said, trying to stay calm as he waved for the waiter. "We'll straighten it out."

"So, Stephie," Aunt Sophie said to Stephanie.

"Do you mind if I call you Stephie?" Aunt Sophie explained. "When you were little, you always called yourself Stephie, and that's how I remember you."

Stephanie tried to smile politely. She hated to be called Stephie. The twins sometimes called her that—but they were only four, so they had an excuse.

"She doesn't really mind," Danny answered cheerfully.

"I don't?" Stephanie cried.

"That's not what she told me," Michelle pointed out. Danny raised an eyebrow, silencing Michelle.

Aunt Sophie went on as if she hadn't heard. "Oh, yes. I remember you quite well," she said to Stephanie. "I remember how you cried because you didn't get the Christmas present you wanted one year. And your father had to give you one of his own just to quiet you down."

Michelle giggled, and Stephanie kicked her under the table.

"And then there was D.J.'s birthday," Aunt Sophie went on, clucking her tongue. "You cried because she got all the presents and you didn't get any. Your father had to buy you something that day too, Stephie."

This was just great, Stephanie thought. Not only

33

was she not hanging out with her best friend and the cute guy they'd met, she had to sit there and listen to embarrassing stories about herself as a little girl.

Worst of all, Michelle was hooting with laughter. Stephanie could see by the look in her eye that she was dying to tell everyone else in the family all about it.

"I just want to remind you of one thing, Michelle," Stephanie said in a low voice. "Before you go blabbing this to everyone else, don't forget about the time you cried because I got to go to the dentist and you didn't!"

Michelle stopped laughing. "You always came home with a little prize," she explained. "How was I supposed to know it was no fun to go to the dentist?"

Their food arrived. Stephanie usually loved Chinese food, but she could hardly relax enough to enjoy the meal. Aunt Sophie fussed through the whole meal. First, she wanted brown rice instead of white. Then she wanted hotter tea. Then her chopsticks broke when she tried to spear one of Danny's shrimp, and she insisted that everyone at the table get new ones.

Stephanie picked at her food. Finally, they were finished. The waiter brought the check and a tray of fortune cookies. There were eight cookies for the four of them. But Aunt Sophie took the plate and handed one cookie to each of them.

"Read your fortune, Michelle," Aunt Sophie ordered. "What does it say?"

"A wise man knows when his plate is full," Michelle read from the tiny piece of paper. "What is that supposed to mean?"

"It means they want you to eat only one fortune cookie instead of two," Stephanie said sadly.

"Stephanie," Danny warned her.

"Sorry," Stephanie mumbled, cracking open her own cookie. "Good things come in strange packages," she read. Stephanie shrugged and dropped the crumpled fortune back onto the table.

"Don't you think you should keep that, Stephie?" Aunt Sophie asked. "You never know. Sometimes there's truth in these fortunes."

Sure, Stephanie thought. *It would be true if it said weird aunts come at the worst time!*

"I guess we're all set," Danny said. He gathered up the doggy bags their waiter had left them. "I'll pay the bill and get the car. I'll meet you ladies out front in a few minutes."

Stephanie and Michelle stood up, but Aunt Sophie stayed at the table. She carefully wrapped the extra fortune cookies in paper napkins. Then she stuffed them into her purse.

"Stephanie," Michelle whispered loudly. "Look what she's doing!"

"Old people do weird things, Michelle," Stephanie said. She sighed as she pulled her denim jacket on and then yanked her hair free of the collar.

"Does that mean I can take those little teacups home?" Michelle asked, gazing longingly at the table.

"No, Michelle," Stephanie replied patiently. "That would be stealing."

She and Michelle followed Aunt Sophie to the front of the restaurant. Aunt Sophie stopped by the cashier and took one of the mints that was sitting by the register in a glass bowl. She chewed it thoughtfully and then smiled. Then she opened her purse.

Stephanie watched in horror as Aunt Sophie grabbed the glass bowl and dumped the entire thing into her bag. Stephanie's face was flaming. *Can they arrest us for this?* she wondered, looking around to see if anyone was watching. Luckily the cute waiter was busy clearing their table.

"Hey," Michelle blurted out as she saw what Aunt Sophie was up to. "Isn't that stealing?"

"Of course not, dear," Aunt Sophie assured her. "The mints are here for customers to take."

Stephanie couldn't remember the last time she'd been so embarrassed. And worst of all, this was a member of her own family. Stephanie wasn't sure how much more of Aunt Sophie she could take. And her visit had barely started!

CHAPTER
4

◆ ◀ ◣ ◆

When they arrived back at the house with Aunt Sophie, Stephanie had never been so glad to get home. The only person there to greet them was D.J.—and Comet. Uncle Jesse was upstairs getting the twins ready for bed. Comet seemed a little nervous—after all, he'd never seen a blue-haired human before. But Aunt Sophie petted the golden retriever happily. "You have a beautiful silky coat, don't you, boy?" she crooned. "Though I suppose it sheds all over the house," she added. Comet wagged his tail at the new member of the household.

D.J. took her aunt's coat. "I think I see a family resemblance, Aunt Sophie," she remarked. "But I'm not sure. Maybe it's your big blue eyes."

"Definitely not the big blue hair," Stephanie murmured.

"What's that?" Sophie asked.

"Uh—I said that D.J. also likes to flirt with waiters. Just like you, Aunt Sophie," Stephanie joked.

Aunt Sophie beamed at Stephanie. "I like a good sense of humor!" she cried.

"Me too," Danny agreed. "So let me go over the sleeping arrangements—because they're no joke!" Danny waited for everyone to laugh. Aunt Sophie smiled. Stephanie, D.J., and Michelle gave him a blank look.

"What do you mean sleeping arrangements?" Stephanie asked. "I think we already know where our beds are."

"But we have to do a little shuffling for guests," Danny explained. "Aunt Sophie will get D.J.'s room, and D.J. will sleep in your bed, Stephanie."

"And where am I supposed to sleep?" Stephanie was almost afraid to ask.

"Downstairs, I think. On the pull-out couch," Danny answered.

Stephanie was in shock. She'd been kicked out of her own room. Out of her own bed! She glanced at the lumpy couch and frowned. *How am I supposed to sleep on that?* she wondered.

First she had to give up her plans for the night,

and now she had to give up her bed. Why couldn't D.J. sleep on the couch? And what about Michelle? It was bad enough that D.J. had her own room and she herself had to share a room with her little sister. Now she couldn't even share the room she hated sharing!

Stephanie took a couple of slow, deep breaths. Finally, she turned to her father.

"Dad . . ." She began in her most pleasant tone. "Not that I mind or anything, but why is it that I get to be the one to sleep on the couch?"

"Well, Stephanie," Danny explained breezily, "Aunt Sophie needs her own room. She is the guest, after all, and that's why she gets D.J.'s room. And D.J. is still studying for finals, so she needs a good night's sleep until all her tests are over. And Michelle goes to bed early, as you know, so she can't sleep on the couch when everybody else is still awake."

Stephanie hated to admit that her father made sense.

"Stephanie, why don't you help your aunt Sophie carry her things upstairs," Danny suggested. "She's had a long flight, and she'll probably want to unpack, take a bath, and get to bed."

Stephanie nodded and began grabbing some of Aunt Sophie's luggage.

"You don't have to carry it all," Aunt Sophie remarked, picking up a few bags herself. "I did manage to get it all here from Europe by myself."

"That's all right," Stephanie grumbled. "I'm used to it."

"And you're probably used to giving up your bed too. It's no fun being the middle child, is it, Stephie?" Aunt Sophie said, cocking her head and looking at Stephanie intently.

Stephanie shrugged. She was surprised that Aunt Sophie seemed to realize how Stephanie felt. It *was* hard being the middle child.

Upstairs in D.J.'s room, Aunt Sophie began unpacking. To Stephanie it looked like enough stuff for a month's worth of vacation. All of Aunt Sophie's bags were open and clothes were spilling all over the place.

"Now, the first thing to do," Aunt Sophie began, "is to clear out some space in the closet. Why don't we move some of D.J.'s clothes to another closet while I'm here?"

"Sure," Stephanie replied. She grabbed an armful of clothes on their hangers. "I'll just put them in my closet. No problem." *D.J.'s gonna love this,* she said to herself.

"Let me take a look, though, before you go," Aunt Sophie said. She came over and peered into

D.J.'s closet. "You know, I'll need some hangers too. Can we switch some clothes from the plastic hangers to the wire hangers so I can use the plastic hangers? I hate to get those little hanger marks in the shoulders of my clothes."

"Sure," Stephanie replied, lifting the stack of clothes she'd just taken out of the closet and putting them back into the closet. "I'll just rehang all those clothes," Stephanie offered, "and *then* move a bunch of them into my closet."

Stephanie started pulling shirts off their plastic hangers and rehanging them on the wire hangers.

"Oh, Stephanie," Aunt Sophie interrupted again. "Do you think you could find a way to move the long-hanging clothes, like the dresses and skirts? And leave the shorter ones, like blouses? I like to have everything hanging the same length. It makes a closet look so much neater. The Tanner family has never been sloppy, you know."

Stephanie sighed and gritted her teeth. "Of course," she replied politely. "I'll just switch all these shirts I've rehung with some of the dresses. And then I'll move them to my closet."

Boy, Dad wasn't kidding when he said Aunt Sophie had the neat-freak genes in her, Stephanie thought. This was more than being neat. This was the eccentric part he'd been talking about.

It took almost an hour to clear out the closet. After that Stephanie found herself in the bathroom, trying to make space in the medicine cabinet for Aunt Sophie's things. Stephanie was juggling three old tubes of toothpaste, Joey's mouthwash, a bottle of aspirin, and a little glass jar of face cream. She had some ancient cough syrup and Michelle's old Mickey Mouse toothbrush tucked under her arm. Then she heard the phone ring.

"Stephanie," D.J. called a second later from downstairs. "It's for you! And it's a boy!"

Stephanie glanced at the junk in her hands and back at the medicine cabinet. It would take forever to get all the stuff back on the shelves without it falling out. She searched for a place to drop everything. She dumped it all into the shower stall and threw a towel over it.

"I'll come back and pick it up after I get the phone," she whispered, pulling the curtain closed. She raced to her father's room and snatched the phone up.

"Got it!" she screamed out.

"Stephanie?" a boy's voice spoke. "Is that you? It's James. Hold on a second, I think I just went deaf."

Stephanie's eyes went wide with surprise. James had called. And he'd called *her*.

"What's happening," James asked. "Your house is so noisy. Are you having a party over there?"

"No, no party," Stephanie admitted. "That's just my family. There are a lot of us. And the phone downstairs is still off the hook. Wait one second."

Stephanie covered the receiver with her hand and screamed again. "Hang up the phone!" There was no way she was going to have someone listen in to her conversation with a boy.

"Listen, I'm just calling to find out if you and Allie still want to go skating. Because my uncle said he'd drive us over to the rink tomorrow afternoon."

"You bet!" Stephanie answered quickly. "After tonight, I really need a vacation."

"A vacation from your vacation?" James asked.

"I guess so." Stephanie laughed.

"We'll stop over tomorrow around two, okay?" James asked.

"That'll be great," Stephanie replied, her heart pounding. "It'll be lots of fun."

"Just don't forget," James said, "I told you I couldn't skate."

The second that James hung up, Stephanie dialed Allie's number. She almost couldn't wait until Allie picked up the phone.

"Allie," Stephanie cried excitedly as soon as she

heard Allie's voice. "It's me, Steph, and I just had the best phone call!"

"Was it Darcy?" Allie asked eagerly. "How is she? Is she going to call me too?"

"Wait a minute," Stephanie said. "The second best phone call then. It wasn't Darcy"—she paused to build up the excitement—"it was James!"

"Oh!" Allie shrieked. "He actually called you! I told you he liked you," Allie said.

"Actually, he called for both of us. His uncle will drive us to the skating rink tomorrow," Stephanie said.

"So—what are we wearing?" Allie asked. Stephanie could hear Allie opening her closet door in her bedroom.

"Hmmm," Stephanie began, "should we go casual-in-jeans? Or funky-and-playful, like *Sassy* magazine? Or should we do some kind of girl-on-ice ensemble?"

"What do you have for girl-on-ice?" Allie asked.

"Maybe something like bright leggings with a big wool sweater?" Stephanie suggested.

"And leg warmers too?" Allie asked.

Stephanie sighed. "Maybe casual-in-jeans is better," she said, chewing on her finger while she considered it. "Maybe we should do jeans and turtlenecks?"

"You mean like J. Crew?" Allie asked.

"Yeah," Stephanie agreed. "You know, kind of rugged and natural."

"I think that sounds good for you," Allie said thoughtfully.

"What about you?" Stephanie asked.

"I'm still considering girl-on-ice," Allie admitted.

"Well, I could do that too," Stephanie said, thinking her oversize red rollneck sweater might be just right.

"Hmm. Maybe not girl-on-ice," Allie said suddenly. "Maybe funky-and-playful is better. You've got those great overall shorts you bought, Stephanie," Allie reminded her. "You could wear those over tights, with a turtleneck."

"Hey, that sounds cute," Stephanie agreed. "I think that's it for me, then. Will you wear the same kind of thing?"

"I don't know," Allie admitted. "Maybe I'll do casual-in-jeans."

"But a minute ago you thought funky-and-playful would be good," Stephanie pointed out. "Now you've changed your mind."

"I know. I just don't want to go looking like twins, you know?" Allie laughed. "You should definitely wear the overalls, and I'll figure some-thing out by tomorrow."

"Do you want to call me in the morning and talk about it?"

"Well, maybe," Allie said.

"Or you could come over and borrow some-thing," Stephanie offered.

"I could."

"Do you want to come after breakfast?"

"Maybe, maybe not," Allie said. "Let me think about it."

"Oh, uh . . . okay," Stephanie agreed. But she wondered why Allie was suddenly being so secretive.

"I'll come up with something great and surprise you. How about that?" Allie said.

"Great," Stephanie agreed. She hung up the phone slowly. She was excited about tomorrow, but also a little confused. She and Allie always discussed what to wear when they went out to-gether. And now she wanted to surprise Steph-anie? That didn't seem like Allie.

Stephanie stared down at the phone and frowned. It wasn't a competition, after all. Or was it?

47

CHAPTER
5

♦ ▼ ◆ ♦

"Up, up, Stephie." The voice rang in Stephanie's ears. "Rise and shine! Time for a hearty breakfast. It's seven o'clock sharp, no time to waste! The Tanner family never sleeps late!"

Stephanie's eyes popped open. Seven o'clock! She was going to be late! She had to shower, and D.J. was probably already in the bathroom.

Stephanie threw off the covers and leapt up. She staggered over to her closet. And staggered. And staggered. And staggered.

Where exactly is my closet? Stephanie wondered through a haze of sleep. *It's usually not this far away.* Suddenly she bumped into the TV, which helped to wake her up completely.

"Ouch!" Stephanie cried out, gazing around in confusion. She realized she wasn't even in her bedroom.

Everything came rushing back all at once. She wasn't in her bedroom because D.J. was in her bed—because Aunt Sophie was in *her* bed—because Aunt Sophie was visiting—because it was Christmas. And that meant no school!

Stephanie grumbled as she headed back for the lumpy pull-out couch. She fell back into the mass of blankets, curled up, and closed her eyes.

"Stephie, Stephie," a high voice shrieked in her ear.

"Stephie, get up!" another voice called into her other ear. It was torture in stereo, and Stephanie didn't even have to open her eyes to know who it was. Apparently her twin four-year-old cousins were awake.

"Alex, Nicky," Stephanie moaned as she felt the little bodies land heavily on top of her. "Can't you see I'm still sleeping?" *Or at least I was, blissfully, just a moment ago,* she thought to herself. But the twins were giggling and jumping all over her. There was no way to get rid of them now. Stephanie poked her head out of the blanket. Immediately a big wet tongue slathered up the side of her face.

"Ugh!" Stephanie cried. She dived back under the covers and wiped her cheek. "Good morning to you too, Comet," she muttered from her hiding place. "Good doggy. Now get lost."

"Come on, boys," Stephanie heard Aunt Becky saying. She felt Alex and Nicky being lifted from the couch. "Okay, Steph," Becky announced after a minute. "It's safe to come out now."

"Time to get up! Breakfast is almost on the table!"

Stephanie heard Aunt Sophie's voice ringing out from the kitchen. Then she heard the heavy steps of the rest of the family heading down to the living room. Stephanie sat up and saw a groggy D.J. and Michelle wander down in their pajamas.

"Aren't we on vacation?" Michelle said with a yawn.

"That's what I thought," Stephanie agreed.

"Come on, everybody," Danny said as he stumbled downstairs himself. "Aunt Sophie likes to eat early. Every day. And since she's offered to make breakfast, it wouldn't be polite to refuse. Personally, I think it's very generous of her."

"Okay, Dad," D.J. muttered. "You can have my share too."

"Where's Jesse?" Stephanie asked Becky. "Isn't he coming to breakfast too?"

"He's brushing his hair," Becky told her.

"That'll take an hour, at least," D.J. quipped.

"Does that mean I can go back to bed for another hour?" Joey asked. He had changed into jeans, but he was still wearing his Bugs Bunny pajama top.

"Sure," Aunt Sophie said. She strode in from the kitchen with an apron on, waving a wooden spoon in her hand. "If you don't mind waiting till lunch to eat. Breakfast is served now—or never. The Tanner family never snacks. Three square meals a day is all anyone needs."

"Since when?" Stephanie mumbled, thinking of delicious afternoon snacks.

"I need someone to squeeze some fresh orange juice," Sophie said, looking over the groggy crowd. "Stephanie!" she cried, pointing her spoon at Stephanie like a magic wand. "That can be your job."

"But we use frozen," Stephanie protested.

"Well, I don't," Sophie replied. "The Tanner family never uses frozen. It's not the same. A little work before breakfast makes everything taste twice as good! Now, come in here and start squeezing. D.J., you can set the table. Michelle, make sure everyone gets their own dish of butter and jam—I just hate people double-dipping their silverware . . ."

I don't know which Tanners she keeps talking about,

Stephanie thought. *Because she sure doesn't know this group of Tanners.*

Stephanie opened the freezer and saw the can of frozen orange juice. She reached for it, but her father caught her eye and gave her a warning look. Stephanie put the frozen orange juice back and, with a sigh, headed for the oranges sitting on the counter.

After breakfast Danny decided it was time for everyone to pick their Secret Santa names for Christmas. Stephanie's hand was so sore from squeezing oranges, she had to ask D.J. to write out a slip for her.

"This is fun!" Sophie cried as everyone gathered in the living room and Danny collected the names in a hat. "I'd love to do the picking!"

"Well," Danny began hesitantly, "I guess that would be fine."

Usually they passed the hat around the room, so each one could pick a slip of paper. Stephanie thought Aunt Sophie should learn this piece of Tanner family custom. "Actually," she began, "it's a Tanner tradition to—"

"Give this hat to your aunt Sophie," Danny finished.

Sophie grabbed the hat and twiddled her fingers

through the slips of paper to mix them up. "Here we go, everyone. Remember to keep it a secret!"

"Joey's hoping he'll get one of the twins," Uncle Jesse announced. "That way he'll have an excuse to spend the whole day at Toys 'Я' Us."

"Just as long as I don't get your name," Joey replied. "Where do you hide hair care products where Jesse can't sniff them out? Last year he found them in Comet's doghouse."

Aunt Sophie handed out the slips of paper. Stephanie was hoping to get D.J.'s name, or Becky's, because she'd seen a great vest that would look good on either one of them. And, of course, the possibility of borrowing it every once in a while made it an even better gift.

Michelle was the first one to be handed a slip of paper. She took it from Aunt Sophie, unfolded it and read it, and then she smiled from ear to ear. It was all she could do to stop herself from jumping up and down.

"Now I know I'll get that stuffed koala bear," she cried.

"What do you mean, Michelle?" D.J. asked.

"I can't tell you. The names we pick are supposed to be a secret," Michelle replied.

"Michelle, why are you so sure you're going to get that koala bear?" Danny asked.

"Could it be that you got your own name on the slip of paper?" Becky guessed.

"But it's supposed to be a secret," Michelle protested.

"Put the name back, honey," Danny said. "Maybe someone else will get you the koala bear."

"Anyway, your stuffed animals are taking over my bedroom," Stephanie pointed out.

Michelle looked crushed as she put the slip of paper back in the hat.

"Hey, there are plenty of koala bears in Toys 'Я' Us," Joey assured Michelle. "Right next to the stuffed llamas."

"You mean you've already been to Toys 'Я' Us?" Uncle Jesse asked Joey.

"Oh, just a little pre-sale mission," Joey said. "Got to be a wise shopper these days."

"Wise?" Jesse asked. "That isn't the word that comes to mind when I picture a grown man drooling over the new King Mojo Komodo toys."

Aunt Sophie gave Michelle another slip of paper and then continued around the room. Finally, she came to Stephanie. "Don't worry," Sophie chuckled, "I saved the best for last."

Stephanie took the small piece of paper and carefully unfolded it. She tried to keep a smile on her face as she read the spidery writing: Great-Aunt Sophie Tanner.

What in the world am I going to get her? Stephanie wondered. *A turbocharged Dustbuster?*

The rest of the day dragged by. First, everyone had to admire Aunt Sophie's souvenirs from Europe. Then her postcard collection. Finally, it was afternoon and Stephanie was in her room putting the finishing touches on her skating outfit. The doorbell rang downstairs.

"Stephanie!" Michelle called up the stairs. "You'd better come down." As Stephanie started down the stairs, Michelle shouted, "Your new boyfriend is here!"

Stephanie almost tripped down the stairs. *Just pretend you didn't hear that, Stephanie,* she told herself. She took a deep breath. She hoped her face wasn't red.

James was standing in the doorway. "Hi!" he greeted her. "Let's go, okay? My uncle is waiting outside by the car."

"So what time are you going to be home, Steph?" Danny asked, poking his head from the kitchen.

"Before dinner," she replied, shrugging into her jacket.

"Well, okay, honey," Danny said, wiping his

hands on a dishtowel. "Have a nice time and call if you need a ride home."

"My uncle will pick us up, Mr. Tanner," James answered.

"Great." Danny smiled. "Now, Steph, just remember to lace your skates tight enough to give your ankles support, but not so tight that they aren't flexible."

"Of course, Dad," Stephanie said, edging toward the door.

"Are you sure you shouldn't take your knee pads and bike helmet, just in case?' Danny suddenly asked. "I can get them—"

"No, Dad," Stephanie said quickly, rolling her eyes. "Thanks, but I'll be careful."

"I'll take care of her, Mr. Tanner," James added with a grin.

Stephanie smiled secretly. She liked the sound of that, coming from James.

First they went to pick up Allie. Stephanie couldn't help but notice how much easier it was for Allie to get out of her house. Allie had on a new pair of charcoal leggings and a teal sweater. "Nice outfit," Stephanie complimented Allie. "It's new, isn't it?"

"Something I ordered from a catalogue that finally got here," Allie said.

Stephanie noticed that Allie was also wearing a new shade of lip gloss, but she didn't comment.

Mr. O'Brien dropped them off at the rink.

"Just remember what I told you," James warned Stephanie and Allie as they got their skates. "I really can't skate very well."

"That's okay." Stephanie sat on a bench and began lacing up. "I'm just glad to be getting out of my house. I finally feel like I'm on vacation."

"Me too!" Allie agreed, already in her skates. "Come on, I can't wait."

"All right," James said nervously as he wobbled over. "But I don't think you two have been listening to me." He stepped gingerly onto the ice. "I'm telling you, I'm just not—"

Stephanie and Allie gasped as James slipped and fell.

"—that great on skates," he moaned, facedown.

"Wow," Stephanie said as she skated over. She grabbed James by the arm to help him up. "You weren't kidding."

"Are you okay?" Allie asked as she took his other arm.

"I am so far," James sighed, brushing off the seat of his pants. "But who knows how I'll be by the end of the night."

"Don't worry," Stephanie said, laughing, "we'll

keep you up. And to think I left the knee pads and helmet at home."

"Hey," James cried in mock anger. "That's cruel."

James wobbled, and before Allie and Stephanie could steady him, he slipped. And this time he brought the girls down with him.

"Now I wish I'd brought the knee pads for me," Stephanie joked.

"Sorry." James grimaced. "I'm sure I'll get better."

Unfortunately, James didn't get better. They made it around the rink a few more times, falling more than anyone could count. Finally, they decided to take a break.

The three of them skated clumsily off the rink and fell onto the benches.

"Ouch," James moaned. "Boy, skating is worse than football!"

When the speed skate was over, a couples-only skate was called. Stephanie and Allie glanced at each other nervously. What should they do? Which of them would skate with James?

"Well, who wants to skate with me first?" James asked.

"Go ahead, Steph," Allie said quickly, looking down at her skates.

"No," Stephanie replied. "You go ahead."

"Maybe I'd better rephrase that," James teased, "since neither of you are jumping at the chance to be my partner on ice. Which of you is brave enough to skate with me?"

"You can go, Allie," Stephanie urged even though she really wanted to skate with James.

"Why don't we do it in alphabetical order," James suggested. He took Allie by the arm. "And don't worry." He smiled at Stephanie. "You'll get a chance to hit the ice with me a few more times."

Allie and James headed back onto the ice and began to make their way slowly around the rink. Without someone on his other side, James had to get a lot of support from Allie. He flung his arm across her shoulder. To hold him up, Allie had her arm around James's waist. The song was one of Stephanie's favorite romantic songs, and she watched Allie and James wistfully.

Did Allie like him? Stephanie wondered as she watched the two of them circle around. It almost looked as if James were skating better. Although Stephanie noticed that he still leaned on Allie for support.

The announcer's voice boomed over the rink. "The next round is for girls only," he called.

Stephanie couldn't believe it. Now she wouldn't

get a chance to skate with James alone! James headed to the snack bar. Allie skated back to where Stephanie was waiting. Stephanie couldn't look at Allie as she glided up to her.

"I'm sorry we skated through the whole song," Allie said at once. "I thought you'd get a turn to skate couples too."

"No problem," Stephanie said, trying to sound casual as she headed out onto the ice. Allie skated right beside her.

"He just seemed to be getting better," Allie continued, "so we kept going."

"I said it's fine," Stephanie replied a little tightly. *Of course he was getting better*, she thought. *You hardly let go of him.*

"Are you mad at me?" Allie asked.

"No way," Stephanie answered quickly. She was not going to make a big thing about it.

"You're not interested in James?" Allie asked, trying to keep up as Stephanie started skating faster. "As a boyfriend, I mean? Don't you still like Kyle Sullivan?"

Kyle Sullivan was a ninth-grader in their school. Stephanie had had a crush on him all year, and Allie knew it. And she also knew that Stephanie and Kyle had never gone out.

"Kyle and I barely even talked to each other the

whole semester," Stephanie answered. "Anyway," she continued, "why do you care? Are *you* interested in James?"

"I asked you first," Allie said quickly.

"Well, then I asked you second," Stephanie replied. Allie shrugged. She and Stephanie skated the rest of the song in silence.

Luckily, when they got off the ice, it was time to meet James's uncle. James didn't seem to notice that Stephanie and Allie were less talkative than before. He was pretty enthusiastic about his success on the ice. All the way home, he kept saying how much Allie had helped him. *Maybe you should hire her as your personal trainer*, Stephanie thought as they dropped Allie off at her house.

"Why don't you come over tomorrow night?" James asked Stephanie as they pulled up in front of her house. "I could play my guitar for you. Or we could just hang out. Tell Allie she can come too."

"That would be great!" Stephanie grinned, waving as James disappeared next door.

Allie may have had the couples-only skate, but now Stephanie had a chance to hang out with James alone. *After all*, Stephanie thought to herself, *He didn't say I had to invite Allie, did he?*

CHAPTER

6

◆ ◀ ◆ ◆

Stephanie raced inside her house. She was really excited over James's invitation. but as soon as she had closed the door, she started feeling guilty. How could she even think about not asking Allie to come? Wasn't the whole point of Christmas vacation to hang out with Allie? Okay, so maybe it wasn't great that Allie skated the whole couples-only song with James. But she probably didn't do it on purpose. Stephanie sighed and picked up the phone. She couldn't hang out with James and not tell Allie. She quickly dialed Allie's number.

"Hello?" Allie answered after a few rings.

"It's me—Steph."

"Oh." Allie was quiet for a few seconds. "What's up?"

"I just wanted to tell you that James invited us over tomorrow night to hear him play music."

"He did?" Allie asked. "Both of us?"

"Of course!" Stephanie laughed to cover up another twinge of guilt. She thought about how she almost *didn't* call.

"That sounds great," Allie said.

"Why don't you come to my house for dinner? We'll go over afterward," Stephanie suggested.

"Sure," Allie agreed. "I'll see you then."

Stephanie hung up the phone and felt a lot better. Allie was really excited. And there was no way that listening to music could be as awkward as skating with three people. Christmas break was definitely back on track.

"So where is everyone?" Allie rushed into Stephanie's room the next night and plopped down on the bed.

"D.J.'s at the library studying for her exams," Stephanie replied. She stood in front of her mirror, finishing the long braid she was putting in her long hair.

"Ugh," Allie shuddered. "That's too bad."

"And Dad's TV station is having some holiday party, so he and Becky and Jesse are going to that.

And Joey's got a gig," Stephanie explained. "The adults are all gone except Aunt Sophie."

"She introduced herself when I came in," Allie said. "She's kind of cute," she continued. "That lime-green color she's wearing really sets off the highlights in her hair," Allie teased. "Actually she looks a little like you."

"What?" Stephanie cried out. "I don't see it. Not one bit. There's not the slightest resemblance between that little blue-haired lady and me."

"Well, how about you if you went punk and died your hair the same color?" Allie teased.

"Yeah, right." Stephanie chuckled. "Though Aunt Sophie is definitely a Tanner. Believe it or not, she's even neater than my dad."

Stephanie spun around and modeled her outfit. She wore a long peasant skirt and a cropped, rose-colored sweater. With her hair in a braid, she looked like she could have been a folksinger herself. "So what do you think?"

"You look great," Allie said, glancing down at her own jeans and plaid shirt. "Now I feel underdressed."

"I'm just excited to be going out," Stephanie said. "And get this—Aunt Sophie actually said she'd be happy to watch Michelle and the twins! Otherwise I would have had to stay home again."

"Then you wouldn't have been able to see James!"

"Exactly," Stephanie agreed. "As soon as we eat, we're out of here."

"Speaking of dinner, what are we having?" Allie asked.

Stephanie checked her watch. "Well, you'll find out in exactly twenty seconds."

"What do you mean?" Allie asked.

"Aunt Sophie says the Tanner family never eats late. She serves dinner at six o'clock sharp," Stephanie whispered. "And six o'clock sharp is exactly five seconds . . . four . . . three . . . two . . . one."

"Stephie?" Aunt Sophie's voice called up the stairs. "Stephanie, you're late! Dinner's on the table. Hurry up now, it's already getting cold."

Allie's jaw dropped.

Stephanie shook her head. "I told you she was worse than my dad."

The girls hurried down to the kitchen. Michelle was at the table, along with the twins, and they all looked pretty glum. Stephanie had a sinking feeling in her stomach.

"Michelle?" she asked quietly. "What's wrong?"

"What *is* that stuff?" Michelle whispered back.

Stephanie noticed that the twins were holding their noses so they wouldn't smell whatever was cooking. She herself had no idea what it was that Aunt Sophie was up to.

"Here we are, everybody," Aunt Sophie sang out as she spun around from the stove with a platter in her hand. "Stuffed cabbage! Delicious and nutritious."

Stuffed cabbage? Stephanie grimaced in horror.

"Don't like cabbage," Nicky whined.

"No garbage," Alex added.

"Cabbage is not garbage," Aunt Sophie said, sniffling. "Besides, Danny loved this as a child."

He would, Stephanie realized.

"Sorry," she whispered to Allie as they sat down. "I guess I should have told you to come after dinner."

Allie tried to smile as she put her napkin across her lap.

"Oh, just a small helping, please," Stephanie smiled as Aunt Sophie approached with the platter.

"One won't make a balanced meal," Aunt Sophie replied. "And the Tanner family never turns down good food."

Who said stuffed cabbage was good food? Stephanie stared as Aunt Sophie ladled three big cabbage rolls onto her plate.

"That'll make your hair shiny, and your skin just like peaches and cream," she said. "Turn all those boys' heads, like that cutie next door." Aunt Sophie winked at Stephanie and Allie, who exchanged a surprised glance. Sometimes Aunt Sophie said things that didn't sound like an "old lady" at all.

"Don't think I'm too old to notice such things, girls. Some things you never outgrow," she said as she sat down.

While they were eating, Danny came into the kitchen with his coat on. He was dressed and ready to go to the station's party.

"Hey, girls," Danny said. He surveyed the dinner table. "Oh, stuffed cabbage! One of my favorites. Too bad I'm eating at the party," he sighed. "Anyway, I just wanted to make sure Aunt Sophie is all right staying home tonight."

"The twins are no trouble," Aunt Sophie assured him. She let out a big sneeze.

"Aunt Sophie?" Danny asked, looking at her closely. "You don't look so well." He put a hand on her forehead, and she brushed it off. "Are you coming down with a cold?"

"It's nothing," Aunt Sophie said. "Just a sniffle."

"Well, a sniffle is the first step toward a cold," Danny said seriously. "You know that. You might have caught it from Stephanie. And the Tanner family never lets a sniffle go unchecked."

Oh, no! Stephanie thought. *Now she's got him doing "the-Tanner-family-never" too!*

"Maybe it's not a good idea for you to stay home with Michelle and the twins by yourself, Aunt Sophie," Danny continued.

"You mean you'll stay home with her? That's nice of you, Dad," Stephanie said quickly. "I know Aunt Sophie would love to spend some time with you. And then you'd be able to sample her wonderful stuffed cabbage—"

"Stephanie," Danny said calmly. "I'm afraid I can't stay home. You know I have to go to the party at the TV station. But since you and Allie are here, why don't you stay and keep Aunt Sophie company?"

"But, Dad," Stephanie cried. "I have plans tonight. Why should I get stuck baby-sitting?"

"I told you how I felt about this visit," Danny replied quietly. "Your aunt Sophie is a guest here, and you're her family. I want you to spend some time with her."

"But I already had to break my plans once before," Stephanie complained. "It's not fair to make me stay home again."

"We've already discussed this," Danny said sternly. "You went out with Allie and James yesterday. I think tonight you can stay in with your aunt and your sister and your nephews."

"But—"

"No buts, Stephanie," Danny warned.

Easy for you, Stephanie thought angrily. *You're going to your party.*

Stephanie turned to Allie and sighed. "I'm sorry, Allie. It looks like James is out again."

Allie's face fell.

"Maybe we can find a good movie on TV," Stephanie suggested.

"Well," Allie said slowly, picking at her cabbage roll with her fork. "Actually, would you mind if I went next door, just for a little while?"

"You want to go without me?" Stephanie asked, surprised.

"Just for a while," Allie said. "Only if you don't mind."

Stephanie couldn't believe what Allie was asking! After all, it was Stephanie who James had invited over in the first place. And it was Stephanie who had shared that invitation with Allie. Wasn't Allie supposed to be her best friend? Wasn't it up to friends to stick by one another in times of great unfairness and hardship—like baby-sitting? If Allie didn't see how wrong it was, what could Stephanie say?

"No," Stephanie said, swallowing hard over the lump in her throat. "I don't mind at all."

Immediately Allie cheered up. She jumped from the table.

"Thanks, Stephanie," Allie said, "you're a real friend. I promise I'll be back in an hour or two."

"Sure, an hour or two. No problem," Stephanie murmured as the front door closed behind Allie.

"Stephie, I'm not feeling so well," Aunt Sophie said. "I think I'll lie down on the couch. Would you watch the twins while I'm resting?"

"Sure," Stephanie replied.

"And I don't need any watching," Michelle added.

"Of course not," Stephanie agreed as Aunt Sophie went into the living room. "You can even help, Michelle. What can we do to keep the twinsters occupied?" Stephanie pointed at her two little nephews.

"Cookies?" Nicky asked, grinning and pushing his plate of stuffed cabbage away from him.

"Good idea," Stephanie agreed as she fiddled with the radio to find her favorite rock station. She turned the music down so that it wouldn't wake Aunt Sophie. Then she pulled out all the ingredients they'd need for the cookies. As Stephanie measured and chopped and stirred, she kept peeking out the window to the O'Briens' house. Maybe she could catch a glimpse of Allie or James. But all she saw were the shadows of bodies moving back and forth in front of the curtain.

The twins put sprinkles on the cookies. Stephanie slid the baking pan into the oven. The phone rang, and Stephanie hurried to answer it.

"Hey, Steph!" Allie cried.

"Allie?" Stephanie was surprised. "What's up?"

"Listen, Steph, I have to ask you something," Allie began. "James isn't the only one who plays guitar. In fact, his whole family is into music. Rock *and* folk music! James is great, you should hear him sing! Anyway, there's this club they all want to go to tonight, and they invited me along, and . . ." Allie took a big breath and blurted out, "Well, if you don't mind, I'd really love to go." She paused for a second. "But only if you don't mind."

What am I supposed to say? Stephanie thought. *No, don't go out and have a great time with a cute guy and his cool and talented family?*

"Of course I don't mind," Stephanie said sadly.

"Really?" Allie almost squealed. "That's great, Steph, thanks. I'll call you tomorrow, I promise."

Stephanie replaced the phone in its cradle and shook her head. She couldn't believe Allie had decided to hang out with James knowing that Stephanie was still stuck at home baby-sitting. An hour or two had turned into the whole evening, and Allie didn't seem to think anything was wrong with that.

Stephanie felt confused. She never thought Allie would have abandoned her like this. *Allie must really be interested in him,* Stephanie thought. *She's certainly more interested in spending time with him than she is with me.*

Aunt Sophie came into the kitchen and walked over to the radio. Without asking Stephanie, she turned the dial until she found some easy-listening Christmas carols.

"There," she sighed, smiling happily. "That's much better."

"Absolutely," Stephanie said through gritted teeth. "My favorite station."

Aunt Sophie smiled cheerfully. "I'm feeling refreshed. All I needed was a little catnap. And now that you're finished with the cookies, you can clean up and we can start on the fruitcake."

"Fruitcake?" Stephanie repeated.

"It's an old Tanner family recipe," Aunt Sophie began.

Stephanie groaned. *Allie's got James,* she thought, *and I'm stuck with Aunt Sophie and a fruitcake!*

CHAPTER
7

♦ ◄ ♦ ♦

"Time to get up!" Aunt Sophie announced from the kitchen. "It's seven o'clock, breakfast is served. No time to waste! The Tanner family never sleeps late!"

This must be one of those repeating nightmares, Stephanie thought as she rolled over and tried to burrow deeper into the covers. *I've definitely had this one before, and very recently.*

"Stephie, Stephie." The high-pitched voices came next.

"Sorry, Steph," Becky's voice mumbled sleepily, and Stephanie felt the twins' bodies lifted off her. "Nicky and Alex seem to be the only ones who are happy to keep Aunt Sophie's schedule."

73

Stephanie sat up on the couch and glanced around the living room. She could hear everyone else in the kitchen, and Aunt Sophie barking out orders. Stephanie swung her legs to the floor and stood up. As she started toward the kitchen she heard D.J. clamber down the stairs. *Wait a minute,* she told herself. *D.J. is downstairs. And upstairs is my empty bed!* The coast was clear! Stephanie hurried up the stairs.

She never thought she'd be so happy to see the room she had to share with Michelle. Stephanie fell onto her bed and pulled the covers over herself. She knew she was missing breakfast, but she didn't mind. It was probably stuffed cabbage omelets! Stephanie happily closed her eyes.

But the next second she was being shaken roughly awake.

"You missed breakfast," Michelle was saying.

"I know," Stephanie murmured happily.

"We had homemade waffles with strawberries," Michelle remarked.

"What?" Stephanie cried, opening her eyes. "Not cabbage omelets?"

"It was delicious," Michelle said matter-of-factly.

"Oh, don't torture me," Stephanie moaned. "If I missed waffles, just let me sleep!"

"I'm going shopping," Michelle continued.

"Aunt Becky's taking me to the mall. Don't you want to come too?"

"Hmm," Stephanie sighed dreamily, closing her eyes and rolling away. "Maybe later."

"Well"—Michelle shrugged—"if you want to stay here, I heard Aunt Sophie say something about making more fruitcakes. And about how the Tanner family never lets a Christmas tree look shabby. I think she's going to take all the ornaments off the tree and clean them." Michelle started walking toward the bedroom door. "I'll just go tell her you'll be around to help."

"Don't even think about it!" Stephanie leapt to her feet and began rummaging through her drawers. "Give me five minutes! I'll be ready to go with you and Becky."

Stephanie grabbed her robe and ran to the bathroom for a quick shower. She wasn't leaving the house only to avoid Aunt Sophie. Though she wouldn't mind missing another fruitcake session. Actually, she still had lots of presents to buy. Including one for Aunt Sophie. And that was going to take some serious thinking. But at least she could shop for Darcy and Allie.

Thinking of Allie made Stephanie feel sad. She still couldn't believe the way Allie had abandoned her the night before. But Stephanie had to admit she was curious about Allie's evening. Especially the part about going out to a club with James and the O'Briens! It was probably a real blast! *So when am I going to be able to do the fun, cool stuff too?* she wondered.

Stephanie finished getting dressed and brushed her long blond hair into a ponytail. Then she ran downstairs to meet Michelle and Becky.

"Just a sec," Stephanie called as she ducked into the kitchen. Her stomach was grumbling and she needed something quick. She searched the cupboard for a Pop-Tart or something, and finally spotted the trays of cookies she'd made with the twins the previous night. They were stuck on one of the top shelves. *Probably Aunt Sophie hid them,* Stephanie thought as she dragged over a chair, *because we all know the Tanner family never snacks.*

"Well, I'm about to break a Tanner tradition," she whispered. She grabbed four cookies from the tray. Stephanie bit into one and smiled. She may have missed waffles for breakfast, but this was a close second. Stephanie jumped down and pushed the chair back to the kitchen table.

"Okay, girls, where do you want to go first?" Becky asked as she and Stephanie and Michelle entered the mall. "The CD store? A clothing shop?"

Stephanie shrugged. "I'm not sure," she said. "I don't have any specific presents in mind yet, so browsing is fine for now."

"Are you sure you don't want to go anywhere special?" Michelle asked Stephanie intently.

"I'm sure," Stephanie replied. "What about you, Aunt Becky?"

"But, Stephanie," Michelle interrupted. "Where would you like to shop? I think we should let you decide."

"Since when are you this nice to me, Michelle? Usually you insist on dragging us to the toy stores, and instead you're letting me decide where to go. What's up?"

"I'm just wondering where would you go to buy a present for yourself, that's all," Michelle said.

"But I don't have to buy a present for myself," Stephanie said. "So why do you want to know?"

"Because I *do* have to buy you a present," Michelle blurted out, then immediately clapped her hand over her mouth. "Oops," she said through her fingers.

Stephanie burst out laughing. "Leave it to you, Michelle. Every year you spill the beans about whose name you picked."

Michelle smiled. "I just want to get you a good gift."

"Thanks. That's really sweet," Stephanie said.

"Well," Becky began, "considering your news, Michelle, I think we'd better split up. What do you think, Steph?"

"Sure," Stephanie agreed. "And, Michelle, if you really want to get me a good gift, start shopping at that Funky Trunk and think vest, vest, vest. . . ."

"That was a pretty good hint, Stephanie," Michelle said. "Just promise one thing."

"What?"

"Promise you'll be surprised on Christmas," Michelle begged.

"I promise," Stephanie chuckled. "How about we all meet back here in a few hours?"

"That's right," Becky added, checking her watch. "We've got to get back home by twelve sharp so we're in time for lunch."

"Or else Aunt Sophie will lock us out of the kitchen?" Stephanie quipped.

Becky couldn't hide the smile twitching at the corner of her mouth. "Okay, okay, she has her 'ways,' but she is a part of the family and we need to respect that."

Stephanie held up her hands in mock surrender. "Just kidding."

Stephanie waved good-bye as Becky and Michelle went off in one direction. Then she turned to start checking out the stores in the opposite direction.

An hour later, Stephanie had scoured an entire department store and was still empty-handed. She had no idea what kind of gift to get for Aunt Sophie. What could she possibly buy for a rule-crazy neat freak? Aunt Sophie probably owned every appliance on the market—or else she'd say the Tanner family never uses appliances when they can do everything by hand.

Maybe a nice sweater? Something to match her blue-tinted hair?

Stephanie's stomach grumbled loudly. She realized she was near the food court. Four cookies wasn't much of a breakfast, and there was still over an hour left before lunch. She was heading for a bagel stand, when she saw a very familiar face. Then another one. Allie and James!

They were sitting at one of the tables. Stephanie watched as Allie laughed and broke her doughnut in two, handing half of it to James. As he took it, Stephanie could see that he had a big grin on his face.

Stephanie ducked behind one of the huge potted plants that circled the food court. Her heart was pounding and her mind was racing. What were Allie and James doing sharing a doughnut together at the mall?

They must have really had a great time last night, Stephanie thought sadly. *Without me.* Such a good time that they'd made another date without her too. And Allie didn't even call to say anything about it. *Probably because she didn't want me to come along. What other reason could it be?*

Stephanie was still lurking behind the plant when Allie and James stood up. James brushed some doughnut crumbs from his lap and ran a hand through his tousled brown hair. He said something to Allie that made her laugh. They picked up their bags and headed off.

Stephanie had to follow them. She hung back, trying to keep some distance between them. She ducked in and out of stores every time it looked as if James and Allie were about to stop or turn around. Stephanie felt awful for spying on her best friend. But she just had to know what was going on. Finally, Allie and James went into a video store. Stephanie paused for a moment so she wouldn't run right into them. Then she followed them inside.

But where were they? The store was packed with Christmas shoppers. And there were so many signs and huge video displays everywhere that Stephanie had trouble seeing through the crowd. She'd lost them!

Stephanie thought she saw James's flannel shirt. She followed it to the classics section. Then she saw it was an older man, about sixty. Definitely not James.

Stephanie whirled around. *Maybe they're in the music section*, Stephanie thought. She hurried down an aisle—and ran smack into somebody else!

"Excuse me," Stephanie started to say before she saw who she'd run into. It was Allie!

"Oh, Steph!" Allie said, her own face full of shock and surprise.

"Hi," Stephanie said slowly. "I didn't know you were coming to the mall today. Why didn't you call me? We could have gone shopping together."

"Oh, well," Allie fumbled, her hands behind her back. "Actually, I just came on my own—"

"Hey, there you are!" James said. "Stephanie, what's up? What a surprise seeing you here too!"

"Well, the mall's a pretty popular place to shop for Christmas presents," Stephanie replied, trying to sound casual. "So it wouldn't have been that much of a surprise if you'd *thought* about it."

"I guess not," James admitted, looking a little unsure.

"I just ran into him here myself," Allie explained—a little too quickly, Stephanie thought.

"Right," Stephanie nodded. "Sure you did."

"Anyway," Allie rushed on, "I've got to get something for my dad at the sporting goods store and James promised to help me, only we've got to do it right away before they sell out, so it was great to see you, Steph, but we've got to go." Allie was backing away down the aisle. "I'll call you later though, okay?"

Stephanie watched them leave in confusion. Did Allie really think that Stephanie would buy that crazy excuse? Why didn't Allie just come out and say *Look, Stephanie, I'd rather hang out with James than with you and we don't want you around.*

Stephanie was really hurt. After including Allie in all her plans, after all the sacrifices Stephanie had made, this was how she was repaid. Some Christmas this was turning out to be!

Not only was she missing out on all the great things she and Allie and James were going to do, but now her own best friend was sneaking around behind her back!

By the time Stephanie got home, her stomach was really growling. She had forgotten to get something to eat. She was so upset about what was going on with Allie, she had to talk to someone.

She grabbed the phone in the living room and dialed. Darcy's phone number at the Aspen lodge was busy. Stephanie kept trying, but she couldn't get through. After half an hour she couldn't ignore the grumbling of her stomach any longer. She hung up the phone and hurried into the kitchen.

"Sorry, Stephanie," Joey replied as he licked his spoon, "all the chicken stew is gone."

"Well, I'll just grab something else, then," Stephanie said, heading for the refrigerator.

"No time for snacks now," Danny said as he came into the kitchen and saw Stephanie rummaging in the pantry. "You can get something at the theater. Today's Tanner family matinee day at the movies!"

CHAPTER
8

♦ ◀ ◢ ♦

"I think you're all going to be very happy with the movie." Danny grinned "We're going to see *The Duck Who Didn't Believe in Santa!*"

"Yay!" Michelle cried. "I love ducks!"

"No way," Stephanie protested, still trying to find something she could grab quickly to eat. "Let's see the new Harrison Ford film. It's supposed to be great!"

"Stephanie, that's not a family movie," Danny explained. *"The Duck Who Didn't Believe in Santa* is for all ages."

"But it's a cartoon!" Stephanie complained.

"It's an animated Christmas special, and it's been very well received," Danny replied, his feel-

84

ings obviously hurt. "Come on now and get your stuff together. You, me, Aunt Sophie, Michelle, D.J., and the twins. And we have to leave in fifteen minutes if we're going to make it."

The phone rang and Stephanie heard Michelle pick it up in the living room.

"Stephanie," she called out. "It's for you. I think it's your new boyfriend again."

Stephanie was so surprised, she almost forgot to be embarrassed. She rushed to the phone wondering why James would be calling her after what she'd seen earlier at the mall.

"Stephanie?" James asked. "Is that you?"

"Hi, James," she replied. "What's up?"

"I was just wondering if you wanted to go to the movies today," he asked. "I know there's something good playing at the mall, and we could catch a three o'clock show if we left now. What do you say?"

Stephanie knew her dad would say no, since he had already decided on a Tanner family outing. And besides, Stephanie had to wonder if the only reason James was calling was that he'd already asked Allie and she couldn't go. *Am I his number-two choice?* Stephanie couldn't help but ask herself. Obviously she couldn't ask him, and she didn't want to tell him she was already hanging out with her family.

"Sorry, James, but I can't go," Stephanie said quickly. "I've already made plans."

"That's too bad," James said slowly. "But I know it was short notice. I guess I'll try and find someone else."

"Sure," Stephanie said, confused again. Did that mean he hadn't called Allie first? Well, now it was too late to change her mind, and Stephanie felt miserable.

The Cineplex was crowded, and there were tons of little kids running around and screaming. Of course they were all going to the animated special. *Great*, Stephanie thought. *Not only do I have to watch a cartoon, I have to listen to a million screaming kids at the same time.*

Stephanie sighed, and scanned the ticket line. But then she gasped. There they were again! Allie was up ahead of her in line with James! Stephanie quickly turned her back and tried to hide behind her family, but she knew it wouldn't matter. If Allie turned around and saw any of them in line, she'd know that Stephanie was probably there too.

Stephanie held her breath as Allie and James bought tickets for the new Harrison Ford action picture and then walked past the concession stand. Whew! Now she wouldn't have to run into them.

Finally I can get something to eat, Stephanie thought as she took her ticket and stared anxiously at the array of candy bars.

"Are you sure you should let them have sweets in the middle of the day?" Aunt Sophie asked Danny. "It isn't really healthy, you know."

"Maybe you're right," Danny began, but when he looked at Stephanie and saw the expression of horror on her face, he quickly changed his mind. "But then again, it is our family tradition to get a snack at the movies, so this time I think it's okay. It is Christmas after all."

Stephanie breathed a sigh of relief.

"Not too much, now," Danny called after them. "You don't want to get sick or ruin your dinner."

"Come on, guys," Stephanie said, quickly grabbing Michelle by the hand. "Let's go before he changes his mind."

"What's up, Steph?" D.J. asked, holding on to Nicky and Alex as Stephanie raced them to the snack line. "You seem in a real rush."

"What can I say, I'm starving," Stephanie admitted, digging in her pocket for her money.

"I have enough for only one thing," Michelle

complained. "Can I borrow money from you, Deej?"

"Sorry, kid," D.J. replied. "I'm broke myself. I spent all my money on pizza and burgers while Kimmy and I were studying."

"Goober!" Nicky cried, running over to the case and pressing his nose into the glass.

"Popcorn!" Alex screeched, pointing at the yellow-filled buckets.

"Stephanie?" Michelle asked sweetly. "Can I borrow from you for a box of Gummi Bears?"

"Sorry, Michelle," Stephanie replied, scanning the counter for what she wanted. "I'm spending all my money on myself. I've already missed two meals today, and if I don't eat soon, I'm going to faint."

"I guess that means we can't get anything for you boys," D.J. said to the twins. "But maybe Stephanie will share."

"Stephie, share!"

Stephanie could feel her stomach growling as she watched the concession girl fill a bucket of popcorn, and stack licorice, Goobers, and Raisinets on the counter for her, along with a large soda.

"No chance," Stephanie said to her four-year-old cousin. She felt bad, but she was too hungry to be generous.

"You look like you're stocking up for the next earthquake," a familiar voice said in Stephanie's ear.

Stephanie was almost afraid to look, but when she did, there was James standing right behind them, grinning at the pile of food on the counter. Stephanie was mortified. *He must think I'm the biggest pig in the world!* she thought.

"Oh, h-hi," Stephanie managed to stutter. Then she introduced James to her sisters and nephews.

"Hi, everybody," James added.

"This isn't all for me, of course," Stephanie said, quickly handing the licorice to Michelle, the Goobers to Nicky, the popcorn to Alex, and the soda to D.J. "I was just kidding about what I said, guys."

Michelle's and the twins' eyes grew big as they took their treats.

"Okay." James grinned good-naturedly. "But it's not any more than I eat all by myself. Anyway," he continued, looking at her curiously, "I thought you said you had plans today and couldn't go to the movies."

"I did say that, didn't I?" Stephanie stalled. "Well, my plans fell through at the last minute, and my family was already coming here, and I figured it was to late to call you—"

"I see." James nodded. "Well, next time, then, right?"

"Right," Stephanie agreed as James moved up to the counter himself. Stephanie was dying to ask him when he'd called Allie about the movie, but she knew she couldn't without sounding jealous.

"Come on, Steph," D.J. urged, snapping her out of her thoughts. "We've got to get to the theater."

Once they were seated, Stephanie tried to get her Goobers back from Nicky, but he held them tightly in his fist. Stephanie knew she'd never get her candy back from either one of the twins. All she could do was watch as Alex gobbled up her popcorn. But it almost didn't even matter anymore. Stephanie had completely lost her appetite. She tried to sit back and watch the movie, but she just couldn't concentrate. And it was so silly, after all. Of course Michelle and the twins were cracking up, but Stephanie couldn't keep her mind off Allie and James.

Finally she climbed over D.J. and the twins and made her way to the aisle.

"Stephanie?" Danny whispered, concerned.

"Just going to the bathroom, Dad," Stephanie lied. "I'll be right back."

Stephanie hurried up the aisle to the exit. She just couldn't sit there and pretend to be interested in *The Duck Who Didn't Believe in Santa*. Not when she had to know what was going on between Allie and James. Were they actually going out behind her back?

Stephanie slipped out of theater number three and casually walked down the hallway toward the rest rooms. She slowed to wait for an usher to pass. Then, after looking over her shoulder and making sure no one was watching, Stephanie slipped into theater six, where Allie and James were

Stephanie stumbled a bit as her eyes adjusted to the dark. But just as she was starting to make out the heads of people in the audience, she recognized the silhouette of a long-haired girl coming up the aisle toward her. It was Allie!

She quickly sat in an empty aisle seat and scrunched down. Maybe Allie wouldn't see her.

But Allie had already spotted her. "Hey, Stephanie," she whispered loudly. "James said you were here. But I thought you were seeing another movie."

"Uh, well," Stephanie muttered. "I am, I mean, I was."

"Well, if you want to watch this movie, why don't you sit with us," Allie said, coming closer.

"But," Stephanie murmured, "I can't . . . because . . . James asked you, not me!"

"But he asked you first," Allie whispered back, "so why should it matter?"

"Because you didn't tell me you were going out with him," Stephanie blurted out. "Just like you didn't tell me you were going to the mall with him. And we've never kept secrets from each other, especially about boyfriends!"

"Shhhhh," they heard loudly from the darkness.

"Stephanie, I don't know what you're talking about," Allie said quickly. "I told you I just bumped into James at the mall."

"Well, you looked pretty cozy to me sharing that doughnut!" Stephanie shot back.

Allie gasped. "Were you spying on me? On your own friend?"

"I wasn't spying," Stephanie replied hotly. "I just happened to see you two together. And you looked awfully cozy. I just wondered why you had so much time to spend with James. You didn't have time for me. Face it, Allie, you abandoned me to go out with James!"

"I didn't abandon you," Allie whispered back, sounding angry herself. "And besides, you said you didn't mind."

"Of course I said I didn't mind," Stephanie replied. "You're supposed to be my best friend.

You're not supposed to ask if you can ditch me for your new boyfriend!"

"Shhhhh," they heard again. "Take it outside, girls, or I'll take *you* outside," the man hissed.

"James isn't my boyfriend," Allie said.

"Well, that doesn't mean you don't want him to be," Stephanie replied. "You obviously like spending time with him more than spending it with me!"

"You're wrong, Stephanie," Allie argued.

"I was wrong about you, I guess," Stephanie replied. "To think you were my friend. Now you're keeping things from me, and sneaking into theaters."

"You're the one who's sneaking into theaters, Stephanie. You're supposed to be in the duck movie right now."

'Well, excuse me, Miss Maturity. I guess you're just too cool for me now that you've got a boyfriend."

"Boyfriend? What boyfriend?"

"The one you're going out with behind my back!"

Allie gasped. "I can't believe you said that."

"Well I can't believe you did that!" Stephanie shot back.

"I guess you should go back to your movie, then," Allie said, close to tears.

"I guess you should go back to your boyfriend, then," Stephanie replied, her throat tight and her eyes wet.

Stephanie stumbled out into the hallway and ran for the bathroom. She thought she was about to explode. She felt terrible. How had that happened? Stephanie didn't know what had come over her in the theater, but she'd been so angry, she couldn't keep herself from saying what she had.

Stephanie hated fighting with Allie. And now everything was all mixed up. She took a tissue from the stall and wiped the tears from her eyes, then stared at her sad face in the mirror. What kind of Christmas vacation was this? Could it get much worse? Darcy wasn't around to talk to, James wanted to go out with Allie instead of her, and Allie wasn't even speaking to her anymore.

After blowing her nose, Stephanie said to her reflection, "I've got no one to hang out with but an old lady and little kids. I don't have even one best friend to talk to."

CHAPTER
9

◆ ◀ ◆ ◆

The next afternoon, the entire Tanner family gathered in the living room, stumbling over each other to look at family photos.

"Oh, it's so fun to get to do this," Becky exclaimed, flipping through the pages. "I love to look at pictures of you as a baby, Jesse. You looked just like the twins."

"There's one big difference between Jesse and the twins though," Joey said. "Jesse was the only toddler in history who ever actually sat still at the barber."

"And here's a picture to prove it," Becky said, pointing to a photo of Jesse looking proud after a new haircut.

"I wish the twins would sit that still for just five seconds," Jesse said. "It took two hours to get the boys to take a nap, which, if we're lucky, might last a whole forty minutes."

"They'd better rest while they can," Aunt Sophie warned. "They're going to have a big night with Santa down at the community center."

"And a big night with Daddy," Jesse added. Later that evening, Jesse and Joey were doing a special broadcast after their usual rush hour show. Station KFLH was broadcasting right from the community center downtown. Lots of little kids would be there, including Alex and Nicky. And they would all want to see Santa Claus.

"Yep." Jesse grinned. "These kids will see me and Joey and Santa—what a night! I really love it when we're broadcasting live."

"Live from Santa's lap!" Joey joked. "Isn't that our tag line tonight?"

"I thought it was live from Santa's workshop," Jesse reminded him.

"Whichever." Joey nodded. "As long as Danny found someone to play Santa Claus. You did, right, Danny?" Joey asked for the tenth time.

"Mr. Thompson," Danny assured him. "The guy who holds the cue cards down at the TV station. And his suit—" Danny began.

"Is in the closet," Michelle finished. "I peeked."

"Just don't let the twins know where it is," Becky said. "If they don't believe in Santa, how will I bribe them into being good?"

"I told Mr. Thompson to come by for the suit on his way downtown," Danny explained. "He'll meet us at the center later, after all the kids have arrived."

"Speaking of kids," Aunt Sophie cried, "I never saw these pictures before!"

Everyone crowded around to look over Aunt Sophie's shoulder. She was pointing to a series of pictures of Danny when he was about four years old. In the first one, he was giving his pet collie a bath. The second photo showed him washing out the bathtub after he'd used it. And the third photo showed him hosing down the driveway.

"Some things never change," Joey quipped.

"Here's one of Stephanie!" Michelle pointed, turning the page. "How old was she then?"

Aunt Sophie checked the date on the photo. "She was about two years old then. And look, she's all dressed up in her older sister's clothes."

"Yep," D.J. agreed with a smirk, "some things never do change. Stephanie's still borrowing my clothes without asking me."

"How do you know I didn't ask you that day?" Stephanie said defensively.

"Because," D.J. argued, "you were only two! You were too young to talk."

"Oh, look at that one!" Michelle cried, pointing to a picture that showed the three girls together a few years earlier: D.J. was leaning over the couch braiding Stephanie's hair, who was sitting on the couch braiding Michelle's hair, who was sitting on the floor.

"That reminds me of me and my sisters," Aunt Sophie said, lifting a hand to touch her own hair. "We used to do things like that together all the time. And I was the middle girl too," she said, winking at Stephanie. "My older sister always got to go out and have fun, and I was always stuck at home taking care of my little sister."

"Sounds all too familiar," Stephanie commented. She hadn't realized that Aunt Sophie was a middle child too. Her father had never mentioned that to her. No wonder Aunt Sophie was so understanding about some of the awful things Stephanie had to endure.

"The older sister and the younger one always get to do the fun stuff," Stephanie pointed out for the benefit of the rest of the family.

"If you call taking final exams the fun stuff,

Steph, you're welcome to sit in for me next time,"
D.J. offered. "I've got a psychology test Monday."

"Hey, Stephanie," Michelle cried, still staring at
the photo of the three Tanner girls. "How come
you don't do this for me anymore?"

Stephanie looked up in surprise as everyone
else laughed.

"What do you mean, Michelle?" Stephanie
asked.

"I mean how come you don't braid my hair and
stuff anymore," Michelle said. "This looks like so
much fun. And I love getting my hair braided."

"Well, Michelle, I'll try to fit more hairdressing
into my schedule, okay?" Stephanie grinned.

"Jesse can give you pointers on that," Joey said.

Aunt Sophie turned a page in the album and
sighed. She held up a picture of Stephanie in her
ballet costume.

"Ah, yes," Danny sighed proudly. "The prima
ballerina. Remember when you used to call yourself that, Stephanie?"

Everyone in the family started laughing.

"I remember at breakfast when you'd try to hold
your spoon with three fingers," Joey reminisced.

"You said that the prima ballerina was always
very dainty, and she ate like a lady and a star,"
D.J. added.

"The prima ballerina!" Michelle grinned.

"I wanted to be a dancer too, once," Aunt Sophie explained. "But when I was younger, we didn't have enough money for ballet lessons."

Stephanie glanced at Aunt Sophie and saw the wistfulness in her eyes. Again Stephanie was surprised. *I guess there's a lot about Aunt Sophie that I don't know,* she mused.

"No way!" D.J. shrieked suddenly, grabbing at one of the photos in the book and hooting. "Look at this," she said, passing the picture to Joey.

Joey took the photo and glanced at it. Then he gazed over at Stephanie and burst into laughter.

"This is great," he muttered, handing the photo to Becky. "Just great."

Stephanie watched with a sinking feeling in her stomach as the photo slowly made its way around the room to her. Everyone was staring at the picture, and then at her, and cracking up.

What could it possibly be? Stephanie wondered, beginning to fume. *Am I wearing a diaper on my head or something?*

Finally, with tears of laughter in his eyes, Danny handed the photo to Stephanie. She was almost afraid to see it. It was a picture of her when she was about Michelle's age, and she was wearing one of D.J.'s bathing suits and pair of high heels. Of course, the bathing suit was drooping off her. Her arms and legs were as thin as twigs. "I don't see what's so funny—" Stephanie began to say.

Then she stopped and peered a little closer. And she felt her face growing hot as she realized why everyone was pointing to her and laughing. The bathing suit was kind of droopy, but something was holding up the top half. Stephanie was mortified.

She had stuffed the top of D.J.'s bathing suit with tissue! There was no denying it. Some of the tissue was peeking out of the suit. How humiliating!

"Well, *I* for one don't see what's so funny about this," Stephanie said. She stood up, feeling mortified. The rest of the family gazed at her and burst into a fresh round of laughter. Puzzled, Stephanie glanced down at herself. *Oh, no!* she thought. *No wonder they're laughing!* Stephanie was standing with her hand on her hip—just like in the picture!

"I *don't* play dress-up anymore," Stephanie insisted.

D.J. shook her head, grinning from ear to ear. "Except with my clothes," D.J. squeaked, which sent the family off in another gale of laughter.

Oh, why couldn't her family leave her alone? Stephanie wondered. Stephanie in her ballerina costume, Stephanie in her big sister's bathing suit—what was the big deal anyway?

"Well, I'm not nine years old anymore," Stephanie burst out. "Michelle is! And I'm stuck sharing a room with her, as if I were a little kid. And now you won't even let me sleep in the room that I can't even call my own!"

"Oh, Stephanie," Danny said, trying to stop chuckling. "It's not so bad—"

"But it is!" Stephanie cried. "You drag me around everywhere as if I were still little, but then you make me stay home and baby-sit like I was grown-up. It's just not fair!"

Stephanie heard the silence behind her as she stormed out of the living room into the kitchen, but she didn't care. *It serves them right if they feel bad,* Stephanie thought. *They never cared about hurting my feelings anyway.*

The phone rang, and Stephanie heard Danny call to her from the living room, "Stephanie! Can you answer that, honey?"

"I have to do everything around here," Stephanie moaned, picking up the phone.

"Hello, is this the Tanner house?" a voice asked before Stephanie could say a word.

"Yes, it is," Stephanie almost growled into the

phone. *And right now I wish I weren't a part of it,* she wanted to add.

"Can I leave a message for Danny Tanner? This is Mr. Thompson."

Stephanie perked up. "The Mr. Thompson who's going to be Santa Claus?" she asked.

"Well, actually, this is the Mr. Thompson who *was* going to be Santa Claus."

"What?" Stephanie asked, confused.

"I'm sorry," Mr. Thompson explained. "I was supposed to come by later on tonight and pick up the Santa suit, but I'm calling to say I won't be able to make it. Something's come up and I'm going to have to cancel on the community center show. Please tell your dad I'm sorry, but I just can't help it."

"I'll pass on the message," Stephanie assured him.

"And I hope he has enough time to find someone else," Mr. Thompson added. "Thanks."

Stephanie hung up the phone and heard a burst of laughter from the living room. *They must be looking at more pictures from the Stephanie Tanner files,* Stephanie thought, immediately feeling sulky again. *Well, I'm not going back in there just so they can laugh at me, thank you very much.* Stephanie gazed around and smiled. Finally, she had the kitchen to herself. Now maybe she could find something good to eat.

Stephanie rummaged through the refrigerator, searching for anything appetizing, but sadly, the only thing she could find was a big bowl covered with tinfoil. And inside was the leftover stuffed cabbage. *Yuck,* Stephanie wrinkled her nose. *No wonder the Tanner family never snacked with Aunt Sophie around, if this is the only thing left to eat.* It seemed as if Aunt Sophie, unlike Stephanie's father, had found a way to actually hide all the snacks. So Stephanie settled for an apple. Not exactly the big score she was hoping for.

Suddenly the phone rang again, and Stephanie cringed. "Might as well get it," Stephanie murmured to herself. "It's not like anyone else is about to," she added sarcastically.

"Tanner residence," Stephanie snapped into the phone.

"Stephanie!" a voice squeaked through the wire. "Is that you?"

"Darcy!" Stephanie cried, suddenly happy for the first time in days. *Finally,* Stephanie thought, *someone to talk to!*

CHAPTER
10

♦ ◂ ▸ ♦

"Darcy, I'm having the worst Christmas ever," Stephanie immediately reported to her friend. "And Allie and I aren't even speaking to each other anymore."

"What! Why not? What happened?" Darcy asked, alarmed.

"Because Allie and I met this great guy named James and we were supposed to do all kinds of stuff together, but it didn't quite work out that way."

"Yeah," Darcy admitted her voice floating back to normal. "Okay. I heard a little bit about it from Allie."

"You spoke to her?" Stephanie asked.

"Last night," Darcy said. "That is, night, my time. Afternoon, your time."

That was when Stephanie had tried to call Darcy too, and her line had been busy. Stephanie had wondered for a moment if Darcy and Allie were talking, but she'd decided that would have been too big of a coincidence. Apparently not. Allie was getting to do everything Stephanie wasn't, including talk to their best friend.

Stephanie was dying of curiosity. "What did she tell you, Darcy?"

"You know," Darcy hedged. "She just said she hadn't been able to see much of you."

Ha! Stephanie thought. *You mean she's chosen not to see much of me!*

"And she told me a little about James," Darcy continued. "About the guitar playing and stuff."

"And she didn't tell you anything about the two of us and James?"

"Not really," Darcy admitted. "I got the impression that she'd spent most of her time with James alone."

"You got that right," Stephanie said. Apparently Darcy didn't know anything about last night's fight at the movie theater. Or that Allie was sneaking around with James behind Stephanie's back.

"But what you don't know is that Allie's been

blowing me off to hang out with him, and when I told her I knew, we got really mad at each other and that's why we're not talking!" Stephanie explained in a rush.

"Wow!" Darcy whistled. "That sounds pretty bad. Two girls and one guy, huh? That's a recipe for trouble if I ever heard one."

"Well," Stephanie admitted, "it's not the guy so much as Allie. She hasn't been a very loyal friend, lately."

"I don't know, Steph," Darcy said. "She sounded pretty unhappy that you two couldn't hang out together like you'd planned.

"Listen," Darcy continued, "I know we've hardly talked, but I have to go now. My folks are waiting for me and I just called to say hello. I'm really sorry about what's going on with you guys though," Darcy added. "I hope it's all worked out before I get back."

"Yeah," Stephanie agreed glumly. "So do I."

"Got to go, Steph," Darcy said quickly. "I miss you."

"I miss you too, Darcy," Stephanie replied as she heard the phone click in her ear.

Stephanie felt a little better when she hung up the phone. *At least I still have one friend out there*, she thought. But then Stephanie realized that she hadn't asked Darcy a single question about her vacation. All she'd done was complain about her own.

"Stephanie?" Danny asked gently when she came back into the living room. "Are you ready to join us again?"

"Yeah, Stephanie," D.J. added. "Are we forgiven yet?"

"I don't know," Stephanie replied. "Are you still laughing at me?"

"Laughing?" Joey cried. "At you? Now, why would we do that? Even if you did look hilarious as a Junior-Junior-Junior Miss America," he added.

Stephanie glared at Joey and he murmured an apology.

"We're all going Christmas caroling," Danny said. "Grab your coat and let's go."

Stephanie shuffled slowly over to the closet. She liked caroling, but at the moment she felt sort of drained of holiday cheer. When Darcy was home, and Stephanie and Allie were speaking to each other, the three of them used to go caroling together. That was a lot of fun, but somehow, caroling with her family seemed like going to the movies or something. The usual Tanner crowd-scene. Stephanie pulled her jacket off the hanger.

"And, Stephanie," Danny added as he put his

own jacket on and bent down to zip Michelle into hers, "you can help Becky with the twins, because Jesse and Joey are heading down to the community center now. The rest of us will go caroling first, then meet them at the center later."

Suddenly, Stephanie stopped getting dressed. *It never ends*, she thought. *Even when I explain how it makes me feel. D.J.'s going caroling, and Aunt Sophie and Dad too. So why am I already designated as the singing baby-sitter?*

"Dad," Stephanie said, hanging up her coat again. "I'm actually a little tired now. Can I stay home, please?"

"But, Stephanie," Danny argued. "It's Christmas. Don't you want to be with us? We're all sorry that we laughed at your picture. But that's no reason not to come caroling. We need your voice, and your spirit."

"That's just it, Dad," Stephanie replied. "I just don't feel like I have any Christmas spirit tonight."

"That's okay, Danny," Aunt Sophie quickly jumped in. "You know, I'm actually not much up to caroling right now myself. You remember that little sniffle I had, right?"

"Of course, Aunt Sophie," Danny said, suddenly concerned. "Are you feeling sick?"

"No, no, I feel fine," Aunt Sophie assured him.

"But I'd like to stay home, and it would be nice to have some company."

"Well," Danny said thoughtfully. "If you want to stay here, I'd rather someone else be here too."

"Thanks, Danny," Aunt Sophie said. "If Stephanie could stay, that would be just great."

Stephanie smiled appreciatively at Aunt Sophie.

"Listen," Danny said, turning to Stephanie and putting his hands on her shoulders. "I really am sorry I laughed at you. And I know everyone else is too. If you want to stay home because you're tired, okay. But please don't be mad at us later." Danny leaned down and kissed Stephanie on the cheek. "We love you, honey. You know that."

"I know, Dad," Stephanie sighed, giving her father a quick hug. "I guess I just need some quiet time right now."

After everyone left, Stephanie fell back onto the couch.

"You may not believe this," Aunt Sophie said, sitting down beside Stephanie, "but I do know how you're feeling."

"I doubt it," Stephanie couldn't help but say.

"Well, like I said, I was the middle girl, too, in my family," Aunt Sophie continued, ignoring Stephanie's remark. "And I always had to give up my bed. Mostly to my sister's girlfriends when they would sleep over."

"Really?" Stephanie asked. *That's no fun*, she thought. *And after four nights on the lumpy couch bed, I should know.*

Suddenly Sophie got a faraway look in her eyes. "I didn't even get my own room until I moved out of the house," she said wistfully. Then she laughed brightly and began, "I remember the time—" But then she looked at Stephanie and stopped. "Oh, never mind. You're not interested in stories about an old lady like me."

"Tell me!" Stephanie prodded, suddenly interested.

Aunt Sophie waved her hand, giggling. "Oh, nothing . . . Well, maybe you *would* like this story. One time I got so fed up with everything at home that I ran away."

"Wow," Stephanie whistled, nodding with approval. "How long were you gone? Where'd you go?"

Aunt Sophie shrugged and gave Stephanie a what-could-I-do look. "Oh, I slept in our old truck that night."

"How far did you go?"

"Oh, well, it was only parked in the driveway.

But I *did* stay there until morning. Gave me a real sense of freedom."

Aunt Sophie started chuckling at herself, and Stephanie found herself laughing along. She couldn't help it. Aunt Sophie could be pretty entertaining sometimes.

"But at least I got out of the house for the night," Aunt Sophie continued, drying her eyes. "And without my parents' permission, I might add. . . . But enough about my boring life. This might be a good time to wrap some presents, while everyone's gone," she suggested. "Go get the wrapping paper and scissors and ribbon and tape. But I like only wide ribbon. And none of those pre-made bows that you buy. We'll make our own. And I hope there's patterned paper, because I do hate to use just plain."

Still smiling, Stephanie went to the closet where the Christmas supplies were stored. She was getting used to Aunt Sophie's demands, and they were even beginning to seem funny in their own way.

"My, my. There's so *much* to do," Aunt Sophie sighed, bustling around the living room and clearing off the table. "And we'll have to find a good place to hide the twins' presents, since they still believe in Santa—"

"Oh, no!" Stephanie cried, leaping back from the closet and clapping her hands over her mouth.

"What's wrong!" Aunt Sophie asked worriedly. "Stephanie?"

"It's Santa!" Stephanie gasped, her stomach suddenly clenching up. "I forgot about Santa!"

"Don't worry, dear," Aunt Sophie said calmly. "Your father found a Santa."

"No, no, you don't understand," Stephanie explained. "He called. Santa—I mean, Mr. Thompson. There was some emergency, and he called to tell Dad that he couldn't make it."

"An emergency?" Aunt Sophie asked, looking concerned.

"And that was hours ago," Stephanie moaned. "But I forgot to tell Dad, and now it's too late to find anyone else to do it. I know it's too late!"

Stephanie paced around the living room frantically. *What can I do?* she thought. *How can I fix this?* Her dad was going to be furious when he found out about the message she'd never given him. And, of course, she'd just gotten angry at the whole family about not treating her like a grown-up! Forgetting an important piece of news like this was definitely not grown-up at all!

"Oh, no!" Stephanie wailed as she realized something else. "All those kids! Nicky and Alex and all those little kids waiting for Santa Claus to show up."

Stephanie stared at Aunt Sophie, feeling panicked.

"Those poor kids are going to be so disappointed, and it's all my fault!"

CHAPTER
11

◆ ◀ ◆ ◆

"Don't worry, Stephanie. The Tanner family never gives up," Aunt Sophie said. "And I think I have an idea. Where's that costume?"

"It's in the closet," Stephanie moaned. "But we'll never be able to find someone to play Santa now! It's too late."

"Stephanie," Aunt Sophie said sharply, "it's never too late. Buck up now, it's no time to crumble. The Tanner family—"

"Never crumbles in a crisis?" Stephanie finished. "I'm sorry Aunt Sophie, but this time they do!"

"You don't have much faith in me, do you?" Aunt Sophie asked as she retrieved the Santa suit from the closet. "Well, I might surprise you. Come on, Stephanie, you've got to help me out. Do you have a pair of black boots?"

"Aunt Sophie," Stephanie said as she watched her plump little aunt shrug into the Santa jacket. "What are you doing? Are you—" Stephanie began. "You mean you're—"

"Don't just stand there. Help me get dressed!" Aunt Sophie ordered. "I'll need some boots."

Stephanie raced upstairs to her room and tore through her closet to find her black Doc Martens. Her heart was pounding. Was it possible? Was Aunt Sophie going to save her from this disaster?

By the time Stephanie got back downstairs, Aunt Sophie had on the Santa wig and beard. Incredibly, without her blue hair showing, she looked pretty good!

"Well," Aunt Sophie asked, her eyes twinkling. "What do you think?"

"You look like Santa!" Stephanie cried happily, handing over her boots. "Are you sure you want to do this?"

"You mean you'd rather let all those little kids be disappointed?" Aunt Sophie asked. "The Tanner family never lets down friends or family. Especially on Christmas."

This time Stephanie thought she'd never heard more beautiful words in her life. She helped Aunt Sophie pull the big Santa pants over her clothes and put a pillow against her stomach. Then Aunt Sophie waddled over to the mirror to check her outfit. When she caught a glimpse of herself, she began laughing with glee.

"Hey, there, I look pretty darn good for an old blue-hair, don't I?"

Stephanie's jaw dropped. Aunt Sophie even called herself an old blue-hair? Now Stephanie was starting to feel guilty about all the mean things she'd thought about her.

"Come on, call a cab," Aunt Sophie instructed. "We've got to get down to the community center right away!"

When they arrived at the community center, the place was packed. Stephanie immediately spotted the table where Jesse and Joey were set up with all their radio equipment. There was a crowd of people around them who seemed to be laughing at one of Joey's jokes.

Stephanie searched the room for her father but didn't see him anywhere. That was a relief. She wanted to get Aunt Sophie in her Santa chair before he asked too many questions.

Stephanie and Aunt Sophie headed for the big chair that was set up at the front. A line of kids stretched away from it and spiraled around the room.

117

"I didn't realize there would be these many people here," Stephanie whispered to Aunt Sophie. "If you hadn't come to the rescue, I would have ruined Christmas for all these kids!"

"Don't think about that," Aunt Sophie said as she placed herself on the ornate chair. "Just think about how many great Christmas wishes I'm going to get to hear!"

"Ho, ho, *ho!*" Aunt Sophie boomed out in a low voice. "Santa's here, so come up and tell me what you want, little ones!"

"Stephie! Stephie!" Stephanie cringed. Nicky and Alex ran up to the chair. Becky was right behind them. Surely, they would recognize Aunt Sophie! Stephanie held her breath and hoped they wouldn't give everything away.

"Hi, guys," Stephanie said. "Who's going to see Santa first?"

Aunt Sophie lifted Nicky onto her lap while Alex stood nearby with Becky. Stephanie could see both boys looking at Santa strangely, but then Aunt Sophie boomed out in a deep voice: "Ho, ho, *ho!* We don't have all day, boys, tell Santa what you want. And you'd better have been *good* too!"

Nicky giggled and Stephanie saw him lean in to whisper to Santa. What a relief! Aunt Sophie's Santa was going to work.

Then Stephanie spotted Danny on the other side of the crowd. When he saw Santa sitting in the chair, he grinned happily and nodded. But as he watched Santa talking and laughing with the kids, his expression became puzzled. When Danny looked around and spotted Stephanie, he frowned, and began walking over to her. Stephanie tried not to squirm.

"Stephanie?" Danny asked her pointedly. "Where's Aunt Sophie?"

"Well, actually," Stephanie gulped. "Do you need to know exactly where she is?"

"Exactly where," Danny said sternly.

"She's exactly . . . where she can do the most good!" Stephanie finally cried. "You know Aunt Sophie. She's a real holiday person. You know the Tanner family never lets a holiday pass without a big celebration—"

"Stephanie!" Danny warned. "No stalling. Where's Aunt Sophie. Is she nearby?"

Stephanie nodded nervously.

"Is she, by some strange accident, wearing a big funny red suit?" Danny asked, his arms crossed over his chest.

Stephanie nodded again, and dropped her gaze to the floor. *When he finds out that I forgot to tell him about Mr. Thompson, I'll be grounded for the rest of my life,* Stephanie thought.

"Are you going to tell me what happened to Mr. Thompson?" Danny asked finally.

"Oh, I can tell you what happened to him!" Aunt Sophie said through her beard, suddenly appearing beside them. "Ho, ho, ho!" She laughed loudly, then winked at Stephanie. She leaned close to Danny to whisper. "He called to say he couldn't make it," she explained. "Some emergency or other. Stephanie and I figured out a way to save the day!"

Stephanie breathed a sigh of relief. She was so glad Aunt Sophie had covered for her. Forgetting to tell her dad Mr. Thompson's message was the worst mistake Stephanie had made in a long time.

"Mr. Thompson had an emergency?" Danny asked. "When? How—"

"And isn't it wonderful that we could help?" Aunt Sophie continued without answering. "What a shame it would have been to let down all the kids, right, Danny, dear?"

"R-right," Danny stuttered. "Of course."

"I should get back to my chair," Aunt Sophie added. "I still have lots of Christmas wishes to hear." She looked over at Stephanie and winked. "And we all want this Christmas to be the very best ever, don't we?"

Stephanie smiled back at her aunt. As incredible as it might have seemed to her a few days ago,

Stephanie was really happy that Aunt Sophie was around. *I really am lucky to know her,* Stephanie realized as she watched Aunt Sophie bouncing a little girl on her knee. *She certainly saved me this time!*

"I can't believe tomorrow is Christmas Eve and I still haven't finished all my shopping," Stephanie moaned the next afternoon. She was packed into the car with D.J., Aunt Sophie, and Becky, who was driving to the mall for a final last-minute shopping trip.

When they got to the mall, Stephanie offered to shop with Aunt Sophie. Even though she knew it would be hard to pick out a present while her aunt was watching, Stephanie really wanted to spend a little more time with her.

Sophie suggested the department store first, and said she wanted to look in the bedding department for a special gift. While Aunt Sophie was browsing, Stephanie wandered over to the jewelry department. She skimmed the glass cases and suddenly her eye stopped on the cutest gift: a pair of earrings that were little gold dangling ice skates—perfect for Allie. Stephanie bought them right away, before she had time to stop and think about it. She didn't want to have to worry about how Allie would get them now that they weren't even speaking to each other anymore.

"Look what I found," Aunt Sophie said from behind her. Stephanie turned and saw her aunt grinning, holding up a Looney Tunes comforter in a big plastic bag.

"Did you get that for Nicky or Alex?" Stephanie asked.

"For Joey!" Aunt Sophie answered. "It'll match his Bugs Bunny pajamas, of course."

Stephanie chuckled and wished for a moment that Aunt Sophie had picked her name out of the hat.

"Now it's time for us to buy our presents," Aunt Sophie announced.

"What do you mean?" Stephanie said, puzzled and curious.

"Well, you should always buy something for yourself too," Aunt Sophie explained, dragging the big plastic bag behind her. "I always do. It's like a reward for making it through the holidays without going crazy!"

At first Stephanie was just surprised. And then she was happy. Somehow, knowing that Aunt Sophie also thought the holidays were crazy made Stephanie feel much better.

"Isn't there anything you want for yourself?" Aunt Sophie asked.

"There is a vest," Stephanie admitted. "I've dropped hints about it to everyone, and I even thought Michelle was going to buy it for me. But Becky warned me yesterday that she hadn't. I've been wanting it forever."

"Well, forever is a long time," Aunt Sophie teased. "And I think Christmas is a good excuse to get what you want, and then we can go get what I want!"

"And what is that?" Stephanie asked curiously.

"You'll see," Aunt Sophie said, looking mysterious.

After Stephanie bought the vest—they had it in her size and it was even on sale—they headed for a shoe store. Aunt Sophie looked like a little kid in a candy store as she pointed to what she wanted in the window.

"Red cowboy boots!" Stephanie cried. Stephanie had been dying of curiosity about what Aunt Sophie might buy herself. *I never would have thought of this,* she thought. *And I still have to think of something that I can get for her!*

"You bet," Aunt Sophie cried gleefully. "I've always wanted a pair of boots like this, and lately I feel young and brave."

Only a few minutes later, Aunt Sophie had another huge package to deal with, along with the comforter.

123

"Boy, dragging these bags around is making me thirsty," she said. "Let's stop for a soda."

They made their way to the food court and Aunt Sophie began fanning herself theatrically as she headed toward one of the counters.

"A drink, a drink, we must have a drink!" she called out to a cute blond-haired boy who came forward to help them.

"Shopping is so exhausting, don't you think?" Aunt Sophie glanced at his name tag. "Ah, Billy," she said sweetly. "What a sight for sore eyes you are. Do you think you could pour me and my dear, *attractive* niece a soda or two?"

Stephanie felt herself blushing. *Oh, no, she's doing it again. I think my aunt has a thing for waiters.*

Billy grinned at Aunt Sophie and turned to Stephanie and winked. "Sure," he said. "No problem."

A few minutes later Billy presented them with a tray of sodas and french fries. "The fries are on the house," he said with a little smile.

"I think that one has his eye on you," Aunt Sophie said to Stephanie as they found a table.

Stephanie laughed. Her aunt was like a teenager sometimes.

"Do you have someone special, Stephanie?" Aunt Sophie asked as she took a sip of her soda.

"Well..." Stephanie began, taking a shaky

breath. How could she tell Aunt Sophie about James. And about Kyle Sullivan? But then she thought about what her aunt had said about being a middle child. And about running away from home. She realized that her aunt wasn't just some old lady who wouldn't understand. She was a real person. She was actually kind of cool. So she explained all about Kyle, who she'd liked all year, and about James too.

"You see, my dear, a Tanner girl never lets only one boy claim her heart," Sophie explained when Stephanie stopped talking. "At least until she decides which boy she wants. It's always smart to play the field with boys. It's your girlfriends that you need to be loyal to."

"But what if it's your girlfriend who isn't being loyal to you?" Stephanie blurted out, thinking about what had happened between her and Allie.

"What do you mean?" Aunt Sophie asked.

Stephanie told her everything that had happened with Allie and James, from the first time they'd met him in front of the O'Briens' house to yesterday's fiasco in the Cineplex.

"It's not that I'm jealous of the two of them," Stephanie tried to explain. "I mean, I don't think I am. I hardly know James, even if I do think he's sweet and very cute. But why wouldn't Allie just tell me if she liked him?"

"Are you sure she does like him?" Aunt Sophie asked. "For a boyfriend?"

"She said she didn't," Stephanie admitted. "But how can I believe her? First she went out with him instead of staying and hanging out with me when I couldn't go. And then she goes with him to the mall, and she never even called to see if I was free. And then she went to the movies with him!"

Stephanie munched on a french fry without even tasting it. "It's obvious that she'd just rather be with him than with me. And it's Christmas vacation, and who am I supposed to hang out with?"

"I don't know, Stephanie," Aunt Sophie began thoughtfully. "Are you sure you're not just upset because Allie has more freedom than you? Which meant that she got to spend time with James when you had to baby-sit, or hang out with your family, or with me?"

Stephanie was silent as she thought about it for a moment.

"I guess I really know the answer to that," she admitted sadly. "Only I think I ruined everything between us and I don't know how to make it up to her."

"Well now," Aunt Sophie chuckled. "Buck up,

girl. The Tanner family never gives up. I'm sure you'll think of something. We'd better go though, or we'll miss our ride home."

Stephanie and Aunt Sophie gathered up all their bags and walked to the entrance of the mall, where they met Becky and D.J.

"Mission accomplished?" D.J. said, looking at all their bags.

"You bet," Aunt Sophie said. "We got lots of good stuff—"

"Wait a minute!" Stephanie suddenly cried. "I still have one more present to buy."

Stephanie dumped her bags with D.J., Sophie, and Becky and ran to the stationery store. She couldn't believe she'd almost forgotten a gift for Aunt Sophie! Luckily, she'd finally thought of just the thing to get her.

Stephanie searched through all the stationery until she found writing paper and envelopes with little pictures of Santa Claus on them. Grinning, she remembered Aunt Sophie in her Santa outfit. The writing paper was perfect. Not only would it remind them both of this Christmas, but—she couldn't believe she was actually thinking this—but now Stephanie and Aunt Sophie would be able to keep in touch with each other, even *after* Christmas!

CHAPTER
12

♦ ◀ ◼ ♦

Stephanie sat on the floor of her room, surrounded by wrapping paper, boxes, and bows. She'd already wrapped the writing paper for Aunt Sophie and the leather belt for Darcy, and now she was measuring paper to wrap the earrings she'd bought for Allie.

As Stephanie took them out of the box again to look at them, she felt a lump rise in her throat. She remembered the first day of vacation, when Allie had hinted to her about wanting new skates. Stephanie and Allie had been so excited about Christmas break, and look what had happened. Everything had gone wrong. And now it was Christmas Eve, and Stephanie hadn't spoken to Allie in days.

Stephanie, Darcy, and Allie had always exchanged presents after dinner on Christmas Eve, but so far Allie hadn't called. *I guess that means she doesn't want to make up,* Stephanie thought forlornly. *She's probably planning to hang out with James.* But even as she thought it, Stephanie realized she didn't care if Allie was with James. All she wished was that things were back to normal and that she and Allie were friends again.

Stephanie gathered up the brightly wrapped packages. She carried them downstairs and placed them under the Christmas tree with all the other gifts.

The phone rang, and Stephanie waited anxiously to see who it was for. *Maybe Allie decided to call after all?* she hoped.

"Dad, it's for you," D.J. called into the kitchen.

Stephanie looked back glumly at the gifts under the tree while her father came out to the living room to take the phone call.

"Oh, hello, how are you! . . . Well, yes, I did get the message," Danny said slowly. "That's okay, everything worked out fine . . . I understand . . . Thanks again . . . Good-bye."

Danny hung up the phone and shook his head.

"That was weird," he said, looking puzzled. "That was Mr. Thompson, apologizing for not playing Santa last night. But he was confused. He said you took the message, Stephanie."

Stephanie gulped and stood up slowly. She knew it wasn't right to keep lying about what had happened the other day. And it wasn't Mr. Thompson who was confused.

"I'm sorry, Dad, but I *was* the one who spoke to Mr. Thompson," Stephanie confessed. "And I was so upset that I forgot to give you the message. Then you left, and it was too late. I almost blew Christmas for all the little kids."

"Well." Danny smiled, walking over to Stephanie and putting his arm around her shoulder. "I know you were upset the other day, honey," Danny said reassuringly. "And I think you had a right to be. After all, you're not a little kid anymore. You really are taking on a lot of adult responsibilities these days, and sometimes I forget to tell you how much I appreciate all the help you give me. And about the Santa thing—no damage done this time."

"Thanks to Aunt Sophie," Stephanie pointed out.

"It all worked out in the end," Danny agreed, "and that's what matters the most. Cheer up, Steph, it's Christmas Eve and the family is together. Isn't that the best we can hope for?"

Almost the best, Stephanie added silently, thinking of Allie. Her dad was right. It was one thing to forget about Santa by mistake, but another thing to forget about the Christmas spirit. She couldn't celebrate Christmas without talking to her best friend.

Stephanie raced up to her room and called Allie's number.

"Allie, it's Steph!" she said as soon as the phone stopped ringing.

"Stephanie!" Allie blurted out. "You're calling!"

"You sound surprised to hear from me," Stephanie said.

"Well, I guess I thought that after the last time we spoke . . ."

"Well, I almost thought so too," Stephanie admitted. "But I just can't stand not talking to you. I want you to know how sorry I am about the whole argument we had. And the whole thing with James—"

"Oh, Stephanie," Allie said. "I'm so glad you called. It was just a misunderstanding, I swear. I really did just run into James at the mall the other day, and I went with him to the movies only because he'd told me you were busy, which is why I didn't call you myself."

"I *was* busy," Stephanie admitted. "Busy being angry and jealous. Of you."

"But you don't have to be jealous of me," Allie explained. "I'm not James's girlfriend, really. The truth is he already has one."

Stephanie let out a little gasp. "He does?"

She could hear Allie laughing into the phone. "Yup."

Stephanie could kick herself. *You mean all this silly jealousy could have been avoided?* she thought. "And when did you find that out?"

"Oh, the other day," Allie replied. "I was dying to tell you, but we weren't exactly on speaking terms. Disappointed?"

Yesterday Stephanie would have been. But what she really wanted to do now was patch things up with Allie, not James.

"I wasn't jealous only because of that," Stephanie explained. "It just seemed like when you had a choice between us, you kept choosing him."

"Oh, Stephanie," Allie began to say.

"But I know that's not true," Stephanie said quickly. "You were just getting to spend more time with James because you had more free time than I did. I was so psyched about all the plans that we'd made together, and when it turned out I wasn't going to do all the things I wanted to do, I guess I got mad that you weren't suffering with me."

"Stephanie, I want to confess something too," Allie replied. "The reason I had to avoid you that day in the music store was that I was hiding your present behind my back and I didn't want you to see it."

"Really?" Stephanie asked, starting to smile. "Then I won't be mad as long as it has Counting Crows in the title."

"Counting Crows?" Allie asked. "But I thought you wanted that Frank Sinatra CD."

"What!" Stephanie cried before she heard Allie cracking up on the other end of the line.

"Just kidding," Allie teased. "Although that was a suggestion from James."

"Well, I'm glad he didn't come between us on that!" Stephanie sighed in relief.

"Since it's Christmas Eve, do you think we should try to get Darcy on the phone too?" Allie asked.

"I'm definitely dying to know what Christmas is like in Aspen," Stephanie admitted. "I bet she's having a great time."

"Hold on a sec," Allie said. "I'll try her."

A moment later Stephanie heard Darcy's voice crackling over the phone line on Allie's three-way calling.

"Hey, you two!" Darcy screeched. "I miss you

133

guys so much!" She paused. "I guess this means you two are talking to each other again. It's really nice to all be on the phone together."

"Yeah, of course we're talking to each other," Allie replied. "And we miss you, Darce. How's the skiing?"

"Pretty great," Darcy admitted.

"And how's Aspen?" Stephanie asked eagerly. "When I spoke to you before I can't believe I didn't ask you anything about you. Like—are there any cute guys around?"

"That's like asking if there are any mountains," Darcy quipped, "or any snow. Every guy in the world who likes to ski is cute!"

"You must be having a blast," Stephanie joked.

"Yeah, do you ever leave the lodge to actually hit the slopes?" Allie teased.

"Sure," Darcy chuckled. Then she paused. "Only, even with a ton of cute guys around, it's not much fun without having you guys here to talk to about them. In fact," Darcy continued, "if I had to choose between spending vacations with cute guys or my friends, I'd pick you two in about a second."

Stephanie smiled, and she was sure that Allie was smiling too. It was funny how Darcy had just put into words what had taken them all of vacation to remember.

"So are you two opening presents without me?" Darcy asked in mock anger. "If you do, I'll feel very left out!"

"No way," Stephanie cried into the phone. "We're waiting for you, like always."

"That's right," Allie agreed. "We'll open our presents when we're all together again."

"Good," Darcy chuckled. "I guess that gives me another week to find something nice to buy for you both."

"*Darcy!*" Stephanie and Allie both shouted into the phone.

"You haven't gone Christmas shopping yet?" Allie asked in horror.

"Just kidding," Darcy laughed. "Listen, I've got to get going. My parents are waiting for me to go down to dinner. Merry Christmas."

"Merry Christmas," they all cried.

Stephanie hung up the phone with a huge smile on her face.

"Honey," Danny said, poking his head into Stephanie's room, "do you want to come down to the kitchen and help Aunt Sophie make her traditional Tanner family eggnog?"

"Sure." Stephanie nodded. "But first I want to tell you something."

Danny arched his eyebrows. "This sounds serious."

"It is, a little," Stephanie admitted, making room for her father as he came over to sit on her bed. "I just wanted to say that I'm really glad that Aunt Sophie came to stay with us." Stephanie sighed. "And I apologize for being so difficult about it."

"It's all right, Stephanie," Danny said, putting his arm around her. "I know that Aunt Sophie is eccentric. And sometimes she's too much of a ..."

"Neat freak?" Stephanie teased.

"I didn't think such a thing was possible," Danny admitted. "But she's still a part of the family. And she's also a very wonderful person."

"I know, Dad," Stephanie agreed. "And that's why I'm glad she came. I really like her a lot, only it took time for me to get to know her, that's all."

"Well, I'm glad you gave it a chance, sweetie," Danny said. "Aunt Sophie lives by herself, but I know that family is very important to her."

"Yup," Stephanie agreed.

"Now I have something I have to admit to you, Steph," Danny said.

"What?"

"You have to keep this a secret though. Just between you and me."

"What is it?" Stephanie urged.

Danny leaned down and whispered in Stephanie's ear, "I hate stuffed cabbage just as much as you do."

Stephanie cracked up. Finally she said, "Don't worry, Dad. Your secret's safe with me."

Danny stood up and walked to the door. "One more thing," he said. "Why don't you invite James to come over later for some of this great eggnog you're going to make."

"Really, Dad?" Stephanie asked happily, already reaching for the phone. "Can I invite his family too?"

"Sure," Danny agreed. "It is Christmas Eve, after all. The more the merrier."

Stephanie quickly got Allie back on the phone.

"Listen," Stephanie said, "my dad just told me to invite the O'Briens over for eggnog."

"Ask them to bring over their instruments," Allie suggested. "That would be really fun and I'm sure they would play a song for you."

"That's a great idea," Stephanie agreed eagerly. "And why don't you come over tonight too!"

"Won't your house be awfully crowded?" Allie asked, sounding unsure for a moment.

"Of course it will be!" Stephanie replied happily. "But you should know by now that this house is never too full for another friend." *Or another family member*, she added silently.

"Okay," Allie agreed. "I'll be there."

Stephanie hung up the phone and grinned. *This is the way Christmas should be*, she reminded herself. Surrounded by friends and family. And next Christmas Stephanie was already planning to invite Aunt Sophie back again personally!

Stephanie hadn't completely blown it. This still could be the absolutely very best Christmas ever. She picked up the phone again and dialed.

"Hey, James!" she said happily when he picked up. "This is Stephanie. You know, I think you still owe me a night of music. . . ."